The Nookienomicon:

Bawdy Tales of the

Cthulhu Mythos

DISCLAIMER: "This is a work of fiction. Names, characters, places and incidents are products of the author's imagination and are used fictitiously. Any resemblance to actual events, locales or persons, living or dead, is entirely coincidental."

Copyright © 2022 Red Cape Publishing
All rights reserved.
Cover Design by Red Cape Graphic Design
Www.redcapepublishing.com/red-cape-graphic-design

CONTENTS

Foreword - HPL Sauce by Tim Mendees

I – The Tower of the Toad by Robert Poyton

II - Re: Annie Mater by S.O. Green

III – The Zann Sextet by Chris Hewitt

IV – Lady Chatterly's Blowhole by Beth W. Patterson

V - Two's Company, Three's A Crowd, A Cult's A Blooming Gangb… by David Green

VI – A Nasty Little Cult by Callum Pearce

VII – The Search for Rhum'pee-Phum'pee by Tim Mendees

VIII – The Bone Room by Ella Ann

Foreword: H.P.L. Sauce
by Tim Mendees

Horror and comedy go together like... to use a British example, a bacon sandwich and a dollop of H.P. Sauce. Throughout my writing career, I've realised that I couldn't write a 100 per-cent serious piece if my life depended on it. There is something that feels so right about wrong-footing the reader by having them chuckling one moment and screaming the next. I feel the contrast not only gives the story time to breathe but is also realistic. After all, some of our funniest quips and moments come in a time of stress. Humour is a coping mechanism, and a major part of our personalities.

As someone of a certain age, I was raised on what many consider the Golden Age of British comedy. The sitcoms, radio sketches and movies made between the tail-end of the sixties and the early nineties are so deeply ingrained in my brain that they are impossible to escape from. I see the world through the lens of *Carry On...* movies, *Fawlty Towers*, *Around the Horne*, *Are You Being Served?* and so many more. I can't look at a fruit and veg stall without concocting a smutty innuendo or risqué double entendre. It stands to reason that it's going to crop up in my writing.

At the same time that I was taking in the rude jokes and slapstick, I was also soaking in the weird and horrific. I'm a lifelong fan of cosmic horror and devour anything I can get my tentacles on. From

The Nookienomicon

Lovecraft, Bloch, Derleth, Smith and Howard all the way up to the writers of the modern day, I'll read anything and everything even vaguely related to the Cthulhu Mythos. For a long time, I have harboured a desire to combine classic British comedy with the expanded mythos of the original Lovecraft circle...

Fortunately, I am not alone.

During the pandemic, when life was conducted over computer screens in varying states of drunkenness, I was fortunate enough to meet various like-minded people during interviews, round-table's and various other zoom-centric events. Whenever Callum Pearce, David Green, Chris Hewitt and myself got together, it was never long before the smutty jokes and cries of "oh, Matron!" were heard echoing around the World Wide Web. While reviewing one of my novellas, Mr Green referred to my mythos as the *Carry On Mendees* universe... thus a seed was sown.

Between the four of us, we hit on an idea too good to ignore. During the course of the thirty mainline titles in the *Carry On...* series, the team lampooned everything from *Anthony & Cleopatra, Hammer Horror* and classic westerns to The British Empire, trade unions and beauty pageants. One thing they never tackled, sadly, was cosmic horror. It seemed, to us, that there was a rich untapped vein of saucy jokes to be mined from the Cthulhu Mythos. Who can resist a good tentacle joke? Giggling like fools, we decided to combine the Golden Age of British comedy with the Golden Age of Weird Fiction. Make a little bit of H.P.L Sauce, if you will.

The Nookienomicon

Next, we needed a few more minds tainted by a love of raunchy comedy to swell our ranks. I'd recently met Robert Poyton, a keyboard player as well as a writer of cosmic horror that is always quick with an organ joke, so he was soon snapped up. Next came S.O. Green, a Scottish writer whose work I always enjoy and has a wicked, some may say twisted, sense of humour. To broaden our horizons, we decided to invite a couple of friends from across the pond who write both horrific and horrifically funny stuff. Ella Ann brings a modern take on the style while keeping to its roots while Beth W. Patterson, another musician quick to talk about her instrument, ups the smut-factor to dizzying heights.

What you hold in your grubby mitts is the fruit of our labours. A love-letter to the giants of comedy and horror alike. The unholy offspring of eight disturbed minds. So, crack open a Party 7, slip off the corduroy pants, get in your favourite beanbag and get ready to chuckle like it's 1979!

Tim Mendees
05/04/22

I

The Tower of the Toad
by Robert Poyton

Kolon the Barbarian grimaced and once again adjusted the heft of his weapon. The fur nappy was a snug fit and more than a little itchy. He tilted his face skyward to take in the full height and girth of the structure before him. Its glossy shaft thrust up proudly into the evening sky, the plum-hued dome at its top glistening in the last rays of the setting sun. The Tower of the Toad, men called it, though few knew why and even less cared. Regardless, Kolon was here to thieve its riches.

He was a young man; black, page-boy haircut framing a youthful face. His body was lean and angular, and he moved with an inbuilt clumsiness, quite often bumping into furniture or tripping over his own feet. But lust burned in his heart. Lust for two things; the great treasure horde rumoured to be within the tower, and the statuesque form of the wizard's assistant. Even as he thought of her, the pulse pounded in his temples and he was forced to pause for another re-adjustment. His mind cast back to the first time he saw that vision of loveliness...

***

"Get out of my way, idiot!" the florid-faced man snarled as Kolon bumped into him. Kolon apologised and turned, tripping over the stall of the

The Nookienomicon

trader behind him. Knick-knacks fell into the mud.

"Oi! What's your game!" the stallholder bellowed, gesticulating. He was a tall man, almost a giant, thick brows knitting beneath a balding pate.

Kolon began hurriedly picking up the items. "Ooh, I am sorry, do forgive me. Here, I'll pick them up." He gathered a handful and straightened, banging his head on the underside of the stall. Placing the pieces of carefully crafted tat back into place, he introduced himself.

"I'm Kolon. From the north. I'm new in town."

The stallholder glanced at the outstretched hand. "You don't say. Well, accidents happen, I suppose." He shook the proffered hand. "I'm Nick. Nick Nack."

Kolon raised an eyebrow. "Nick Nack?"

"Yes." The man placed beefy fists on his hips.

"And you sell... knick knacks?"

"I do." Nick's brows were knitted again. "Got something to say about it?"

"No, no," Kolon attempted a hearty chuckle. "It's, er, lovely... very nice."

The fists uncurled. "Well, that's alright, then. Tell you what, trade is quiet today, let's nip into the Queen's Legs over the road. You can buy me a drink."

Kolon glanced over his shoulder at the shabby looking inn. "Oh. The Queen's Legs open, then?" he asked.

Nick gave him a leer. "Well, you'd have to ask the King, wouldn't you?"

Guffawing heartily, the two new friends crossed the muddy, reeking street to the tavern beyond.

TIM MENDEES
CREATOR OF NIGHTMARES

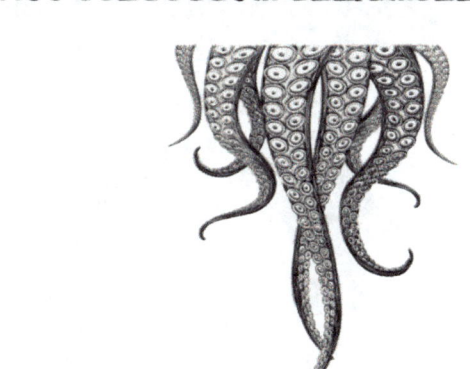

TIMMENDEESWRITER.WORDPRESS.COM

The Nookienomicon

***

The inside of the tavern was no less decrepit than its outside. A variety of dubious individuals lounged at tables, leaned shiftily against walls or, in one case, slumped in a puddle of something foul on the floor. They stepped over the snoring form, Nick smiling at the dour figure behind the bar.

"Good day, bar keep," Nick called cheerfully. "A tankard of finest ale for me and my friend, here."

The squat figure put down the filthy cloth he'd been wiping a flagon with and, grunting, pulled on the pump handle before him.

"That'll be a silver talent. Each."

The frothing tankards were banged, slopping, onto the bar and the pair lifted, clinked and supped. It was then that Kolon saw her.

A vision entered the taproom. A statuesque blond, hair piled high, her tight-fitting, shimmering green gown accenting her natural curves. She wiggled to the bar, placing two large ewers on the stained counter.

"Fill 'em up, Charlie. The usual," she requested, her voice music to Kolon's ears.

He turned and looked down at her. "They're big jugs," he stammered.

She gave a laugh like the pealing of bells. "Ooh, cheeky!"

Kolon flushed and stammered some more. "No, I didn't mean that, I meant…"

But she was already leaving, the jugs filled to the brim with wine.

The Nookienomicon

"Who is that?" he asked his companion, not taking his eyes off the woman as she walked back towards the door.

"That's Blue Sonya," Nick replied, emptying his flagon with a gulp.

"Blue? But she's dressed in green. Why is she called Blue?"

The answer came as a burly market worker patted Sonya's backside as she passed. The diminutive form span and unleashed a torrent of invective upon the man that would have curled a docker's toes. Kolon gasped. Not only did he learn several new words, he learnt a couple of other things too, one of which, he thought, was physically impossible. If anything, he was even more impressed.

"Where is she from?" he asked, turning back to Nick now that Sonja had left.

"Don't even think about it, lad. She's the wizard's assistant. She lives with him in the tower."

"Wizard? Tower?"

Nick rolled his eyes. "Uttah Smutt. He lives in the Tower of the Toad." He eyed the empty flagon meaningfully. "Are you getting another round in, or what?"

***

Nick had been reluctant to say any more about the wizard or the tower, so the next day Kolon began making enquiries. Most city dwellers, it seemed, shared the trader's attitude, refusing to answer his questions. It was not until late that

The Nookienomicon

afternoon when, having stopped in a shady tavern named The Olde Cock, he got more information.

A sign outside proclaimed "Tonite, the Return of the King! Elvish Greatest Hits!" Inside, amid the murk and smoke, a white-clad, pointed-eared singer crooned on a small stage in the corner. He wore blue suede pointy shoes and was singing something about "shake, rattle and troll" to an audience whose indifference lay across the room almost as heavy as the fug. A large, scarred individual was seated at a table, drunkenly boasting to all in earshot.

"I'm the best thief around, I tell you. Why, I'd steal anything from anyone, no matter how well guarded. Save, perhaps, the Tower of the Toad."

The man turned in his seat at Kolon's touch on his shoulder.

"I would hear more of this Tower. Tell me of it."

The big thief squinted up at him in the dim candlelight. "Why, every child knows that it's the abode of the wizard, Uttah Smutt. They say he is a sorcerer! A nookiemancer of great power who has amassed a fortune in gems."

"Why is it called the Tower of the Toad?" Kolon asked.

The man shrugged. "Don't know. Don't care."

"And who is this wizard, exactly?"

"A powerful man, not to be trifled with. Some tell of a prince who once irked the sorcerer, who tried to command him to carry out some task. The wizard became so angry, he snapped his fingers and turned the prince into an egg!"

"An egg?"

"An egg! And as if that wasn't enough, they say

The Nookienomicon

he then took him home and boiled him for tea!"

"These riches, why has no-one stolen them?"

The burly figure stood now, peering down at Kolon through a shaggy brow. "Are you dumb, lad? There is the wizard, plus who knows what guardians. Who could find a way?"

"Seems a way could be found, if it be coupled with courage." Kolon's eyes narrowed to slits now.

The thief roared, "Away with you, bumpkin," and shoved Kolon halfway across the room. The barbarian's temper snapped.

"You would insult me and then lay hands on me?" The sword whipped from its sheath and the room erupted. In the press, the sole lantern in the room was knocked over and extinguished. By the time it was re-lit, the thief lay dead on the floor, stabbed through the heart to the awe of the crowd. Few could know that the thief had, in fact charged at Kolon, who slipped in a puddle of ale and fell forward, his opponent impaling himself on the outstretched blade.

***

And so it was that the young barbarian now found himself staring up at the impressive tower. It was circled by a wall, scarcely taller than a man. It was to this he quietly jogged, sword gripped between teeth, jumping up to grab the parapet. He pulled himself up and rested atop the lintel. Before him lay a well-attended garden, with hedges, low trees and fine lawn, lit in the soft glow of several sconces. He dropped silently to the sward below. A

The Nookienomicon

noise had him wheeling, poised to strike. A rustle of bushes presaged the appearance of a looming figure in the gloom.

"Kolon?" came a familiar voice, the figure moving forward into the torch-glow.

"Nffwl? Whll foo fffar ffer?" The young thief removed the sword from his mouth. "Nick! What are you doing here?"

"I might ask you the same, young man."

"I've come to steal the jewels, and to woo Sonja. And you?"

The big man chuckled. "Wooing, eh? Is that what they call it these days? I'm here for the jewels, too. For I am not Nick Nack, market trader. That is just a cover for me to case this joint. I am, in fact, the renowned master thief, Nick Fings." He bowed.

"Nick Fings?" Kolon raised an eyebrow. "You are a thief, and your name is Nick Fings?"

"Yes, what of it?" Nick folded his muscular arms.

"Erm, nothing. So, what now?"

"Let's work together, lad. I'm sure there's enough jewels for two inside."

Kolon nodded and gestured to the garden. "It's a nice place he's got here."

"It is," replied the burly thief, touching the nearby foliage. "I do like a nice, trimmed bush."

Kolon was about to speak again when Nick stilled him with a raised hand. "Don't move!"

A low shape slunk towards them across the lawn, the menacing form of a great lion!

"Crums!" Kolon invoked the name of his northern god. "That thing would eat me whole!"

The Nookienomicon

Nick shook his head. "No, I think they spit that bit out. Stay behind me and hold your breath!"

Kolon did as bade while Nick rummaged in his sack, producing a blow pipe. He put it to his lips and puffed a cloud of yellow dust towards the advancing beast. As it drew closer, Kolon could swear it was cross-eyed. In any event, the powder did the trick. The great cat screwed up its face, turned and fled.

"What was that? The dreaded yellow lotus?" the young man asked.

"No," Nick replied. "Sneezing powder." Sure enough, the sound of cat sneezes faded away into the night. "Come on," prompted Nick, "to the tower!"

Minutes later, they were at the foot of the great shaft. Looking up revealed a balcony's edge high up, just below the dome. Nick rummaged again, producing a long rope and grapnel. Stepping back, he swung three times and released, the grapnel flying high up to catch on the lip of the balcony. He grinned at Kolon who examined the slim rope doubtfully.

"A quick tug?"

"There's no time for that. We need to climb."

Kolon grunted. "Is this rope made from the tresses of dead women, steeped in the sap of the ulbas tree to strengthen it?"

Nick frowned. "No. I bought it from the local hardware store. Friend of mine owns it."

"What's her name, Sellia Nails?" Kolon enquired.

"Don't be silly. It's Ron. Ron Ronnie. I said I

need some gear for a job. He says, "do you, Nick?" I says I do Ron Ronnie, I do Ron Ron. So, he sells me four candles and this rope." Nick displayed the candles in his sack. "Enough chat, let's climb."

***

The two men set to and many minutes of sweating and grunting later, they made the balcony, slipping over its low edge. The balcony circled the tower, the plum-coloured dome now directly above them. There was only one door. Nick stroked his chin.

"Go and check over the edge, make sure there's no guards in the garden."

Kolon thought this strange but complied. Nothing moved below. By the time he turned back, Nick had gone in through the door. Kolon waited, unsure if he should follow or not. Before he could make up his mind, the master thief reappeared. Pale he was, and slack jawed. Blood dripped darkly to the white stone. He stretched a hand to Kolon then slumped slowly to the floor.

Kolon swore and, sword in hand again, prodded the door open with its tip. Peering in, he saw a large, circular, lit chamber. It was empty save for a few chests and a trapdoor at its centre. Kolon edged nervously towards it. There was a strangely familiar scent in the air that he could not quite place. A sound brought him spinning round. As he did so, his foot slipped in a pile of white mess and he fell heavily. The action saved his life, for over him hurtled the huge, terrifying form of a giant chicken!

The Nookienomicon

With a squawk it leapt for him, claws extended. The wickedly curved talons hit only air as they sailed above him and Kolon rolled to one side before scrabbling frantically to his feet.

Now began a grim game of cat and mouse. The chicken, wary of this new prey, slowly circled the perimeter of the room. Kolon, sword extended, did likewise, both maintaining eye contact. Fate intervened again, as Kolon banged his shin on a chest, one of many strewn around the chamber. It was at that moment the foul fowl decided to strike. It sprang forward with a disembowelling peck, but Kolon was no longer there, he had bent to rub the damaged limb. The chicken, unable to change course, flew past him and out of the open doorway, there to plunge over the rail of the balcony. Kolon heard a wild squawk, the brief flapping of useless wings, and a dull thump. With a sigh of relief, he sheathed his sword and moved to Nick's side.

The old thief was clearly close to death. He clutched the front of Kolon's tunic, his voice dry and hoarse. "Who'd have thought it," he croaked. "Me, the King of Thieves, done for by a dirty great clucker! Get the treasure, lad... get the girl..." His voice faded into nothing and Kolon stood, swearing revenge. Ignoring the chests, he headed straight for the trapdoor in the centre of the floor. It lifted to his touch, revealing a spiral staircase winding away below. Sword in hand, the barbarian trod the steps, pausing only to rub his head after banging it on a low beam.

The stairs ended in the centre of another large chamber with a domed golden ceiling. The walls

The Nookienomicon

were lined with tapestries, the marble floor partly covered by thick rugs. The scent of exotic incense floated up from a brazier on a golden tripod, and behind it sat an idol on an ebon plinth. Kolon stared in horror. The image had the vague outline of a corpulent man, but the head was pure madness. Too large for the body, it had all the features of a toad. The wide mouth, the pendulous jowls, the rounded dome of a head. The face was incredibly lined, what little hair it had was greying and crinkled. The eyes were closed, the thing appeared to be carved of jade. Kolon strode carefully forward, gaze fixed on the motionless idol. Its thin legs were crossed beneath it, hands folded in its lap below the rotund belly. The eyes suddenly snapped open. This was no idol; it was a living thing - and he was trapped in its lair!

The heavily lidded eyes examined the man before them. The tip of a tongue flicked briefly over a flaccid lip. The creature shifted its bulk, noisily breaking wind.

"Oops. Sorry about that, mate. It's the diet, you see? They feed me nothing but boiled cabbage, ruinous on the digestion. Still, it's a tidy little bird brings it up to me. A right little cracker, wahahahaha!"

The thing's ribald laugh sent ripples across its belly. Kolon was shocked out of his stupor.

"But - but - you're alive? You're a... a thing?"

"Yes, mate, of course I am. Saag Nosha's the name."

"I'm Kolon. Pleased to meet you."

"Kolon, eh? Well, you'd know all about digestion, I suppose."

The Nookienomicon

"What?"

"Never mind." Saag raised an eyebrow. "Anyway, what are you doing here? A tea leaf, are you? Come for the gems?"

"Yes, something like that. Where you from then? I've not seen anything like you before."

"You wouldn't have, would you. I'm from beyond. I'm a Great One."

"You're not looking so great right now."

"Well, it's no wonder, is it? Trapped in this place, fed on boiled cabbage. Come to this plane, Uttah Smutt says. You'll have a lovely time. Wall to wall virgins, he said. And what do I get? Boiled cabbage." As if to punctuate the point, there was another parp of escaping gas.

Kolon waved a hand in front of his face. "I'm guessing when it comes to virgins, you're in the wrong city. But why did he want you here?"

"Power, lad, power. Us Great Ones possess the secrets of sorcery, see?"

Kolon wiped the spittle from his tunic. "Sorcery?"

"Sorcery. Old Smutty was under a curse. These wizards constantly feud amongst themselves and he'd gotten into a fight with a fellow from the East. An old fakir."

"So not a real wizard, then?"

"Oh, he was real enough. Boobi Chod. He placed a curse on Smutt. It meant he had to walk everywhere on bare feet, had poor bone density and truly awful bad breath."

"You mean -"

"Yes. Old Smutt was a super-calloused fragile

The Nookienomicon

mystic hexed by halitosis."

There was a pregnant pause. Kolon coughed and continued.

"So you lifted the curse, then?"

"I did. And he was supposed to let me go. Instead, he trapped me on this plane, bound me to this chamber and regularly pumps me for information."

Kolon pulled a face and stepped back.

Saag Nosha was speaking again. "But you could help me out. There's a way to break my chains. All you have to do is kill me…"

***

Kolon warily entered the guard chamber. As Saag had promised, the guards were slumped over their table, loudly snoring. Passing through, Kolon trod along a corridor to the thick, ebon door at its far end. Holding his breath, he grabbed the handle, twisted, pushed and charged into the room, only to trip over the edge of a rug and crash to the floor, his sword clattering away. Through the clouds of incense, he looked up to see the figure in repose on the silken chaise-longue suddenly spring up and advance towards him. A thin man, clad in shimmering turquoise robes, hand held up, fingers poised to cast a deadly spell. This must be Uttah Smutt! The wizard, nostrils flaring, curled back a thin lip and sneered.

"'Ere, what do you think you're doing? How did you get in here?"

Kolon attempted to regain his sword, composure

The Nookienomicon

and dignity. He stood up, sword thrust aloft. His helmet slipped down over one eye.

"I am Kolon the Barbarian," he exclaimed.

"Careful," Uttah responded, motioning to the sword. "You'll have someone's eye out with that. Anyway, stop muckin' about, tell me how you got past the guards."

"They are all asleep!" Kolon grinned.

Uttah tutted. "Typical! You just can't get the staff these days. And every wizard needs a good staff. I was just saying to my friend Sorriman the other day, you know, you just can't - but what am I telling you all this for?" He turned, beckoning to a shape in the corner. "Butch! Butch! Kill!"

The recumbent canine rolled onto its back and lifted four paws into the air. Uttah's nostrils flared even wider. "See what I mean? It's a disgrace. Spent a fortune, and what do I get? A sub-woofer. He's a special wizard's dog, too."

"Is he? What breed is that then?"

"He's a labracadabrador."

Kolon winced, then remembered why he was there. "Look, you just stay there, right? Come closer and I'll chop you in half with me sword!"

Uttah raised his eyebrows. "Well, you do have a big chopper, I'll give you that. But this is my tower! I'm in charge here! I'm a renowned wizard, I'll have you know! I was even asked to contribute to the Nookienomicon!" He thrust his hands up again, the sleeves falling back to reveal skinny arms. But before he could let off a cantrip, Kolon spoke again.

"Not anymore! Saag Nosha bade me give you this." He rummaged in his tunic and threw a curious

The Nookienomicon

yellow object on the ground before the sorcerer.

Uttah Smutt recoiled in distaste. "Is that what I think it is?"

Kolon nodded. "Yes. And Saag instructed me to say he gives you a last gift and a last enchantment."

Uttah was pale faced now. "But that's his… that's his…"

Kolon, now feeling pleased with himself, chuckled. "Yep. All I've done is follow the yellow dicked toad."

The wizard's disgust turned to fear and he clamped a hand to his forehead. "Woe!" he cried. "Woe! Woe is me!"

To Kolon's surprise, the figure of the wizard grew fainter and fainter. The high-pitched voice likewise faded, until, with a faint phut, Smutt vanished completely, leaving a stupefied barbarian staring into empty space. Kolon glanced at the dog. The dog glanced back, turned over and went to sleep.

"Smashing," he said, sheathing his sword and rubbing his hands together. "Now, where's that Blue Sonya?"

He found her in the next chamber, the wizard's laboratory, dusting an alembic.

"Ooh, hello," she smiled, turning, feather duster in hand. "Where's old Smutt, then?"

"He disappeared with a small poof," Kolon explained.

"Only a matter of time," she replied. "Anyway, what are you doing here?"

Kolon attempted his best grin. "I've come to take you home. I like taking experienced girls home."

The Nookienomicon

"But I'm not experienced."

"You're not home yet."

"Ooh, cheeky!" she giggled, waving the duster. She took the barbarian's arm as they exited the tower.

***

Kolon was very pleased with himself. True, he had no treasure, but he'd avenged his friend and had a beautiful girl on his arm. As he looked back, he saw the tower sag and droop, as though all the stiffness had gone out of its stone walls. Then he looked forward, to the road and inn ahead and to the night's pleasures which awaited. What Kolon didn't know though, what he couldn't know, was that Blue Sonya had been serving the wizard for a long, long time. It was his magic that had kept her looking so young for the past ninety-five years, and now that the wizard had faded, so would the spell. Still, he'd find out in the morning…

II

Re: Annie Mater
by S.O. Green

When I first met Annabelle Mater, she was responding to an advertisement I had posted in the Arkham Gazette. My research into the reanimation of corpses was reaching its fruition, you see, and I needed a capable assistant to see it finished. Unfortunately, my previous assistant, Holden, had left on an expedition to Innsmouth with a male colleague from Miskatonic University, and had written recently to tell me they had married and settled there (though he neglected to mention who they had married).

Thus, I found myself in need of a new understudy. I first saw Annabelle seated in the waiting room of the former dentist's office I had appropriated for my work. The frosted door had been recently painted to read, 'Hector the Body Erector'. Literally everyone who walked through it—or even just knocked on it—asked what I meant by that. Strange that none of them could connect it to my research.

I was immediately struck by Annabelle's professional appearance—the short, fashionable bob, the pressed blouse and slacks, the well-manicured fingernails, particular on her index fingers. Her typing fingers, I presumed. And, when she rose to shake my hand, I detected a firm grip. She had admirable wrist strength.

The Nookienomicon

"You realise that this isn't a common profession for a lady?" I asked her, once introductions had been made.

"Well, that's fortunate," she sniggered. "No one ever accused me of being a lady."

"You may find my experiments quite shocking. There will be a lot of blood."

"What's a little blood between friends?"

I nodded. The fact that she wasn't squeamish was in her favour. My experiments could be harrowing at times, but we were going to change the world for the better, I was sure.

"The aim of my research is nothing less than the total resurrection of a dead human body. I wish to make reanimation a reality. You, as my assistant, will be required to arrange for chemical deliveries and a fresh supply of cadavers, as well as assisting me in the operating theatre."

"Oh, so you're saying that you need my help getting the stiffs up? Well, I don't have a lot of experience in that area, but I'm game to try anything once."

"Speaking of which, I must ask if you have a medical background. Do you have any experience of human anatomy?"

"Absolutely! Mostly female anatomy, if I'm being honest."

"So you were a gynaecologist?"

"In a manner of speaking."

"Were you employed at Arkham General?"

"No, I was…freelance. Anywhere I could find an opening really. You know how it is."

I nodded, but I didn't. Ever since my time as a

The Nookienomicon

student at Miskatonic University, I had been working exclusively towards the perfection of my process for reanimating the dead. I had taken no other posts. Still, Annabelle seemed to have a good work ethic and I approved.

"Have you ever held a position of authority?"

"I can hold more or less any position. I'm quite flexible."

Bemused by the statement, I pretended to make a note on the typed resume she had presented me with and gave a nod.

Her credentials weren't perfect, I will admit, but she seemed both enthusiastic and motivated. There was also the small matter that she was my only applicant, which made the decision much easier.

"I suppose my final question for you is, when will you be able to start?"

"Right away, of course," she said brightly. "I don't need to give any notice to my current clients. Actually, they usually prefer if I surprise them with a visit. So, I'm free for whenever you need me."

"In that case, I think I will need you tonight."

Annabelle laughed and, at my raised eyebrow, said, "Sorry, you just sounded like one of my clients for a moment there. Tonight sounds fine. Are we going grave-robbing or...?"

"No, I think we'll save that for another night. This evening, I have an appointment at an establishment in the Red Light District. I don't imagine you know of the place."

"Actually, I know it quite well. Can we pay a visit to the Witch House on the way? I have a...friend who dances there."

The Nookienomicon

"No time for visits, I'm afraid. There is a specific gentlemen's club I must attend—the Silver Moonlight Lounge—that may hold the answers I seek."

"You know that's a...gentlemen's club in the very strictest sense of the word, right? As in, 'no women allowed'."

"I will need you to wait in the car."

"Just out of curiosity, what is it you think they do at the Silver Moonlight Lounge exactly?"

"I imagine they drink brandy and discuss philosophical matters. Obviously, I disagree with the chauvinism in a 'no women allowed' policy, but they are a very old-fashioned institution."

"Yes. Old-fashioned in the Spartan sense, I imagine."

With her duly hired, and with her first week's pay granted in advance, Annabelle collected her coat and made to leave. I'd heard stories about the Red Light District—it had a reputation as a seedy and criminal place—and I worried about taking a sweet, young woman like her with me, but I needed the forbidden knowledge possessed by the Silver Moonlight Lounge and I would probably need a driver, in case the alcohol overcame me.

"I will pick you up tonight. May I ask where you are currently residing? I notice that your resume doesn't include an address."

"Oh, that's because I'm staying at a boarding house on Mill Road run by a Mrs. Palm. I don't have the money for a room of my own, so I...cohabit with her five daughters Monday to Friday, and Mrs. Palm herself has me at the

The Nookienomicon

weekends."

It was a curious arrangement, I was forced to admit, and all I could think of to say was, "That's very generous of them."

"Even if I don't have any money, I try to pay them in services where I can."

"I imagine it must be difficult to get a good night's sleep in a different bed every evening."

At this, she laughed. "You're telling me. I'm exhausted!"

***

That night, I collected Annabelle from the boarding house. She was standing outside, smoking, and didn't notice me until I peeped the horn.

"Is something on your mind?" I asked, as she settled herself in the passenger seat.

"Wednesdays are my favourite," she said, and I didn't understand so I simply drove.

We made our way through Arkham, towards the Red Light District. She said very little, and I assumed it was apprehension about our destination. I was apprehensive too, but when we turned the first corner, into the infamous pool of scarlet light that bathed the entire neighbourhood, I realised this wasn't a menacing or unfriendly place. Quite the opposite, in fact - the men and women I saw all seemed very friendly indeed. Annabelle smiled and waved as we drove past, and I wondered if she knew other people who worked here.

"Could I get you to drop me off?" she asked, as we drove past the gaudy sign for the 'Witch House',

The Nookienomicon

which featured an exceptionally detailed woman's silhouette wearing a pointed hat.

"Unfortunately, I did bring you here in an official capacity. I may need you to drive me home in the event I need to drink to ease the transaction at the Silver Moonlight Lounge."

She nodded. "I've heard it's easier after you've had a drink, yes."

The Lounge wasn't difficult to find. Devoid of the district's usual friendliness, the building was cold and austere on the outside, and a man in a tailored black suit stood in the doorway, a buffer of stiff formality against the carnival colours and arched eyebrows all around. I found myself wondering why the men of the Lounge had made their base here.

Hidden in plain sight, I supposed.

"I won't be long," I said, as I parked.

"I've heard it doesn't take men very long anyway."

"Yes, we tend to be more efficient. Business-like."

"Plenty of the women back there seemed business-like to me."

I left her at the wheel and made my way into the Lounge. The man at the door frisked me, paying particular attention to the usual hiding places, and I was permitted to enter. Were they expecting danger? I suppose they must. They held many dark secrets there, and Arkham had a reputation for breeding cults in the basements and back alleys who longed for that information. Who knew what madness they might unleash if they ever penetrated

The Nookienomicon

the Lounge and manipulated its members?

Inside, I found a sumptuous lounge—more gaudy, more hedonistic than I was expecting—where men of all ages sat about drinking brandy and smoking cigars. Here and there, they paired and walked away to the backrooms, presumably to discuss more private and delicate matters. I imagined all kinds of vital issues must have been settled here. The fate of the world, entrusted to these fine intellectuals.

I had no time to mingle. I asked the servants where I could find Doctor Brunton, the owner of the lounge, and told them that I had an appointment. A rather stiff young man led me to a room in the east wing — Brunton's office, I assumed — and announced me at the door.

I'd expected to find Doctor Brunton seated at his desk. Instead, he was lying on a large, four-poster bed with his chin propped on his fist, wearing a dressing gown of fine silk. He was middle-aged, but had his hair and beard neatly trimmed. I think he was also wearing eye shadow.

The servant drew the door shut behind me and Brunton patted the bed beside him. "Come and join me, there's a good fellow."

I nodded and obeyed. I was aware the Silver Moonlight Lounge must have been founded on strange customs that predated modern ideas of etiquette, but this seemed highly irregular. I racked my brains for historical civilisations that had conducted their business in bed.

"I'm afraid this isn't a social call, Doctor," I said, as I slumped, fully clothed, on the sheets beside

The Nookienomicon

him.

"Even so, you could take your jacket off and make yourself more comfortable. In fact, feel free to take off as much of your clothing as you'd like. There are more robes on the pegs by the door."

"That's very kind of you, but I'm actually here regarding a problem. You see, for years I have been working to perfect a process to reanimate the dead, but to this day, whenever a dead body arrives at my office, I haven't been able to…"

"Get it up?"

"Well, yes, actually."

"I've helped a lot of men with similar problems. Have you considered a drink beforehand? Perhaps a gentle massage?"

"I've tried all manner of things, in all kinds of combinations. I feel like there's a limit to the chemical processes I've used. I think I might require…eldritch assistance."

"So you've come looking for a performance enhancer, is that it?"

"In a manner of speaking. Does the Lounge have anything that might help me?"

"Oh, I could help you with all kinds of things," Doctor Brunton said, and lay a hand on my arm. When I continued to stare at him, uncomprehending, he sighed and climbed off the bed. "But I think I have something that will help you with your 'reanimation' problem."

He drew my attention to a bookcase across the room, from which he drew a well-maintained but inconceivably ancient tome. Was it made from human skin? Or just something that looked like it?

The Nookienomicon

Either way, someone had grafted a face into the cover, and it was frozen in a look of perpetual scandal, as though it had glimpsed something tremendously rude.

"Here it is. The Nookienomicon. This is sure to get them up. But you'll need to be careful with the spells and rituals detailed within. You might get more than you bargained for."

I reached out to take the book. "Thank you, Doctor. I think the world will be a better place after this."

"Certainly more interesting," Brunton said, then pulled the book away. "Of course, I'll need something in return. A service, if you will."

"What did you have in mind?"

His eyes glittered. He lay the book down on the desk and produced a pair of crystal orbs from a drawer.

"I'm just going to do a little scrying, but these get awfully heavy, so it's good to have someone to hold them for me."

I nodded. "I think I'll need two hands."

"That's what they all say."

***

When I returned to the car, I found Annabelle in the driver's seat. Clutching the Nookienomicon tightly, I slipped into the passenger seat, and only then noticed the three women sitting in the back.

"I told them I'd drive them home," Annabelle explained cheerfully. "I mean, it's not right, is it? Poor, young girls wandering the streets at night.

The Nookienomicon

Someone should be looking out for them to make sure they don't get into trouble."

"That's very charitable of you. I suppose I can loan you the car, if you drop me at my office."

"I was hoping you'd say that. So, what's with the skin book?"

"This is the Nookienomicon. Doctor Brunton of the Lounge believed it was the answer to my…problems."

"Yes, I was talking to the girls about that. They said it happens sometimes, but mostly they just need a cuddle and to be told everything's alright, and sometimes the problem just fixes itself, if you know what I mean."

"I don't think this is a problem that will fix itself. I think it will take…forceful measures."

Annabelle shrugged. "Nothing wrong with that under the right circumstances. Pursuant to consent, of course."

A couple of the girls behind me giggled. I assumed they'd just remembered a joke. I was too eager to return to my office and learn the secrets of the Nookienomicon to pry.

"What did they ask for in return?" Annabelle asked, as she put the car into gear.

"He asked me to cup his balls."

"Seems fair. How was it?"

"They were quite cold at first, but they warmed up quickly. And he said it aided his concentration. We both learned a great many things from the experience, I'd say."

"That's nice. Tonight seems like a night for learning things, doesn't it?"

The Nookienomicon

She looked in the rearview mirror, and I assumed she was checking for traffic behind us. There were an awful lot of vehicles in the district, but most of them were pulled over to the side of the road. I found it all very unusual.

We made small talk all the way back to my office. At one point, I asked one of the girls how her business was.

Her response, "If I had another pair of legs, I'd open up in Boston," confused me greatly.

Mostly, Annabelle and her friends talked about going back to her boarding house for dinner, and I wondered how her hostess would feel about her having so many visitors all at once. Annabelle also talked about a cat, but she hadn't mentioned owning a pet.

I excused myself, eager to begin reading, and she apologised in advance if she was late for work the next day.

In truth, I didn't mind what time she arrived. Our real work wouldn't begin until nightfall.

***

I pored over the Nookienomicon late into the night. Much of the wisdom contained within was lost on me, not because it was written in a strange, alien language, but because I couldn't interpret the references. Many of the rituals involved incantations intoned while grasping rods of power or drinking from divine chalices, but how did one obtain these items?

At some point, I must have succumbed to sleep

The Nookienomicon

at my desk. I dreamed strangely, of faces yet unseen and voices yet unheard. I saw Annabelle reading the book, one eyebrow raised, and realised that she understood it far better than I.

I saw the truth. If I were prideful, I would never succeed. My assistant stood a better chance of bringing my experiment to fruition than I ever would. It needed to be her.

Beyond that, I saw only glory, and recalled a face I had not thought of in years. That stern and statuesque sentinel of the Miskatonic University dormitories, who had put fear into the hearts of the students and kept even the professors and postgraduates in line with her iron will. At that time, I had no idea of the role she would play in my undertaking.

I woke with her name upon my lips.

"Oh, Matron."

***

"This all seems quite straight-forward to me," Annabelle said, after a few minutes perusing the Nookienomicon.

"Really? I couldn't make head nor tail of it."

She laughed at my choice of words. "I think that's what you're *supposed* to make of it. It's not that surprising though. You're very…straight."

"I try to uphold principles of integrity and the scientific method, if that's what you mean."

She looked at me, and the glint in her eye turned, for a moment, to sympathy. "No, that's not what I mean at all. Anyway, it looks like there's a ritual for

The Nookienomicon

reanimating the dead here, but it mentions that there'll be…side effects. The resurrected will be, erm, quite stiff, according to this."

"Well, rigor mortis might have set in, so I suppose that's not so surprising. Will it ease in time?"

"Assuming the dead man 'visits with his widow or some other accepting female', it says here."

"I see," I said, even though I didn't. Annabelle seemed distracted, so I imagined she understood, even if I remained confused. "Does it mention where someone might find this 'other accepting female'?"

"I wish. No, I'm assuming it's up to the resurrected man and us to make that happen. Maybe we should start with the easier option and find a man who was married?"

"That shouldn't be difficult. I will speak to my contact at the mortuary."

"That's right. I forgot you've been at this for quite a while, haven't you? Alright, well, you make those arrangements. I have some things of my own to do."

"Like what?"

"The ritual requires a large amount of…energy. A specific type of energy. So I'm going back to the boarding house. Hopefully the girls haven't left yet."

"How will they help?"

Annabelle laughed and tucked the book under her arm. "The same way they helped me last night, I imagine."

The Nookienomicon

***

Arkham Mortuary was an old, Gothic building crouched at the edge of an ancient and dreary cemetery, like a giant gargoyle covered in smaller gargoyles. Pine trees carpeted the surroundings in a thick blanket of needles and the moon was suitably eerie that evening, wearing a shroud of gauzy cloud.

In the dense forest, I could hear the lowing of some wild animal. When I mentioned this to Annabelle, she only winked and said, "Those wild animals must be having a really good time."

We waited in the car for my contact to signal us. It still smelled of perfume from Annabelle's friends and she was smoking again, so the air was warm and hazy.

"Did you collect the energy we need?" I asked.

"We went through the ritual two or three times, just to make sure," she explained. "So I think we should have enough to help you with your performance issues."

"Excellent. Then we can begin just as soon as we have access to the mortuary. We'll have to move quickly to avoid being seen. We'll creep around the back and go in as quietly as we can."

"Easier said than done, from what I've heard," Annabelle muttered. "Couldn't we just negotiate our way in through the front? I'm sure I could manage it with a little coaxing. I've never had trouble before."

"No, I think I'd prefer to take the back door."

"It's fine. I respect everyone's preferences. Did you at least bring protection?"

I nodded and moved my jacket aside, revealing

The Nookienomicon

the handle of the snub-nosed revolver tucked into my pocket. Dealing with reanimated cadavers could be messy work. They were inhumanly strong and mindless, though I hoped to rectify that issue tonight.

"Hopefully, it will be big enough," I muttered.

"Men care too much about things like that," Annabelle said. "Honestly, it won't count for much if you don't know how to use it. So my friends tell me anyway. I don't care much for things like that myself."

"Do your friends have much experience handling weapons?"

"They have experience handling all sorts of things. Nimble fingers."

A light winked on in the downstairs window. It flickered once, twice, then went dark. I popped the car door.

"That's the signal. Remember what we talked about."

"Going in through the back door and using protection," Annabelle said. "Got it."

We crossed the overgrown lawn and found the back door unlocked, as expected. Inside the gloomy confines of the mortuary, my contact, Douglas Graves, awaited us. He had a sombre, grim demeanour that suited a man of his profession.

"The man you requested is downstairs," he said, without so much as a word of greeting. "Naked and under a sheet."

"He is dead, isn't he?" Annabelle asked.

"Yes, and quite recently too," Douglas insisted. "I made certain of it."

The Nookienomicon

Annabelle shuddered. "Remind me not to come here ever again, especially when I die."

"This way, please."

Douglas took up a hooded lantern and led us down into the bowels of the mortuary. The air took on an eerie chill and I thought I could feel the dread hand of some strange, supernatural entity hard at work. What that hand was doing was a matter of conjecture.

Douglas seemed like he wanted to watch the process, but Annabelle just stared at him until he left. I set down my bag and began to place and light the candles we had brought. I had wondered at their place in the ritual, but Annabelle had insisted things like this needed the correct 'mood'. I also chalked the markings from the Nookienomicon on the tiled floor, though some of them reminded me of graffiti I'd once seen in a bathroom somewhere.

Our 'patient' was a relatively young man who'd still somehow died of heart failure. The official report, according to the paperwork Douglas had left me, stated the cause of death as 'exhaustion'. I wondered if he'd been a marathon runner.

"Are you able to read the incantation?" I asked Annabelle, as I completed my preparations.

"It's written in a language I can't get my tongue around, and that's saying something because I've been told my tongue's quite talented."

"Is that so?"

"My friends always described me as a cunning linguist." She grinned. "Fortunately, there's a translation in the margin, so I think we'll be just fine."

The Nookienomicon

She proceeded to the head of the table. I left the body covered. I didn't want the sight of a cadaver to unsettle her delicate sensibilities. She took up a pose like she was on stage and began to recite from the translated ritual.

"*Ancient gods, with powers eternal, we call upon you to engorge this vessel with new life.*"

"That's an odd turn of phrase," I said.

"Maybe it's a mistranslation. Wait, there's more. *We beseech you, enter this vessel now and bring it to the climax of resurrection. Take this energy we have gathered, harnessed from the rhythm of true life.*"

"The heart?"

"Something like that. *Take this energy and make this vessel live again, so that it may finish what is unfinished, fulfil what is unfulfilled and satisfy what is left unsatisfied.*"

"That seems slightly vague."

"Actually, I think I know *exactly* what it means."

At this point in the ritual, I believe the incantation began to take effect. There was *definite* movement under the sheet, around the central region of the cadaver. Annabelle blushed and lifted the book to cover her eyes.

"Arise!" she commanded, and the body took evident notice. "Arise!"

An errant gust of wind—quite improbable in a sealed basement—blew out every candle and our lantern. With a great groaning noise, I heard the cadaver throw itself off the mortuary slab and stumble to the door. I hastened to relight the lamp and lifted it to find that our dead body had indeed arisen, and it had left its sheet behind.

"After it! Quickly!"

I led the charge up the basement stairs, Annabelle close behind, clutching the Nookienomicon to her chest. The face on the cover must have been apoplectic at this point. There was a scream from above and I redoubled my pace, only to find Douglas cowering on the floor at the open back door.

"Heavens, man, you're white as a sheet."

"You would be too, if you'd seen what I saw!"

"I got the gist of it down in the basement," Annabelle said. "I can see why you'd be intimidated."

"This has been a thoroughly hair-raising experience," I said.

"It wasn't his hair being raised I had a problem with."

"We need to find our runaway corpse, before something terrible happens."

"I don't think we need to worry too much about that," Annabelle said. "I know exactly where he's going."

***

Mrs. Letitia Ryder—for after the death of her first husband, she had reverted to her maiden name as being somehow more 'suitable'—had inherited her estate at a young age. She had gone on to marry twice more, and twice more tragedy had struck. Annabelle and I had intervened in the second tragedy, and had now perhaps brought on a third.

The Nookienomicon

I hesitated to call on a bereaved woman on such an ominous night, but if there was a chance our escaped cadaver was here, menacing her, we needed to know.

I checked my pistol again and stepped out of the car.

"Give me a moment to firm up my resolve."

Annabelle nodded. "It's always a good idea to firm up before going in."

Together, we marched up the gravel path and rang the doorbell. I prayed that things hadn't taken a turn for the worse.

It took a couple of minutes before a shape appeared in the frosted glass, staggering in the light from the hall. For a moment, I feared someone had been seriously hurt. Then the door opened, and a dark-haired woman wearing a silk bathrobe and not a lot more leaned out into the night. There was a cigarette between her lips and what looked like steam rising from her collar.

"Good evening, Mrs. Ryder," I said, bowing my head.

"Good evening, Mrs. Ryder!" Annabelle said, with significantly less decorum than I.

"Forgive me for the delay, but I wasn't expecting visitors. I'm afraid you…caught me in the midst of something."

"We're sorry to intrude, madam, but—and this may sound like an odd question—has your husband come home this evening?"

"My dead husband?"

"The very same."

"Well, this may sound like an odd answer, but

The Nookienomicon

yes, he has come home. He's upstairs as we speak, and he seems quite eager for me to return. I think he missed me."

"It didn't strike you as strange that he'd somehow returned to life?"

"For a moment, but then I saw something that took my mind off it, and I haven't really had the time to think about anything else since. I've been…occupied."

"Does he seem…well?"

"Does he seem well-what? Honestly, he seems to be in perfect health. Better even than he was before. He's… How to put it?"

"Animated?" Annabelle suggested.

"Yes. Expansively so. And do I have the two of you to thank for this good fortune?"

"We are merely scientists, madam," I said, "pushing the limits of what can be achieved. Your husband is, hopefully, the first of many to be revived. I am hopeful there will be more like him."

Mrs. Ryder sucked her cigarette until the filter caught fire and then tossed it away. "Yes, that sounds like very worthwhile research you're doing. How can I repay you?"

I opened my mouth to insist that no payment was necessary, but Annabelle spoke first.

"Perhaps you and I could discuss payment together at a later date, Mrs. Ryder. I know you're probably eager to return to your husband, but we could arrange a private meeting, the two of us, at your pleasure?"

Mrs. Ryder arched an eyebrow, and I was glad that they seemed to be getting along so well. While

The Nookienomicon

I hadn't begun my research with the intention of making money, additional funds would help in the procurement of materials. At the very least, we'd need more candles and chalk.

"I should probably run some tests on your husband," I said, "just to be sure nothing's wrong with him. Besides the obvious, of course."

"That can wait until morning," Annabelle said. "I'm sure he has his hands...very full with Mrs. Ryder. We should probably take our leave before he comes for you."

"You mean, before he comes for me *again*?"

"Yes, and we'd hate to interrupt any more than we already have, so we'll just leave you to...get back to it."

Annabelle dragged me away from Mrs. Ryder's sprawling manor house by my sleeve. She vanished back into the confines of her stately home to reconvene with her husband. I hoped that their reunion would be fulfilling for them both. Annabelle certainly seemed to think it would, as we returned to the car.

"Seems to me, this is perfect. He can't very well die of exhaustion now, can he?"

***

The subsequent weeks were a flurry of activity, as we began our research in earnest. Mrs. Ryder, it turned out, was an ideal patron. She spoke of our work to friends, family and, in fact, anyone who would listen. We were suddenly inundated with requests from recently bereaved widows wishing us

The Nookienomicon

to restore the vigour of their partners.

Having perfected the ritual, I undertook the work alone, leaving Annabelle to console the women for their losses. She made many new friends, and made quite regular follow-up appointments with them. All of them described their returned spouses as 'attentive', 'energetic' and, on several occasions, 'masterful'. Annabelle seemed to know exactly what this referred to.

And so I had, in the end, triumphed over death. More than that, I had made quite a successful business out of it. The sign painted upon my door had been repainted in gold leaf, and now read, 'Hector South: Reanimator'. Annabelle had taken out an ad in the Arkham Gazette, the same newspaper that had caused us to meet in the first place, offering our services.

She even went so far as to add 'satisfaction guaranteed' at the bottom. With so many of our patrons seeming extremely, even breathlessly, satisfied, how could we claim otherwise?

But there was one bit of news that threw a pall over this. I remembered fondly my time at Miskatonic University, and had the greatest respect for the woman who had ruled over the dormitories with an iron fist, our formidable matron, Titania Delarge. While admiring the advertisement that proclaimed me as 'the Reanimator', I caught sight of her obituary and realised she had passed.

I sighed and set the newspaper aside, "Oh, Matron…"

"What's the matter?" Annabelle asked, looking over. She craned her neck to see the photograph that

The Nookienomicon

accompanied the grim news. "Someone you knew?"

"Yes. A fine figure of a woman."

"I can see that. How tall was she exactly?"

"In excess of seven feet, I think."

"Wow, so they'd be exactly at eye level."

"What would?"

"Nothing, I was just thinking out loud. Were you close?"

"No one was close to Matron. She was a hard woman. Stern and authoritative. Many were the unwary boys of Miskatonic University who earned her ire with their shenanigans and felt the lash of her tongue."

"Oh, to be an unwary boy of Miskatonic University…"

"Honestly, it's a shame you won't have the chance to meet her. She was a singular woman."

"I like it when they're single, that's true. But, you know," Annabelle said, and her voice took on a conspiratorial tone, "there *is* a way I *could* meet her."

***

Douglas arranged our visit to the mortuary, as per usual. Even so, there was nothing 'usual' about this. Our first woman patient, and for it to be *this* woman…

It was all too much.

I thought I might faint, so I asked Annabelle for time to catch my bearings. She graciously agreed and skipped gaily downstairs to 'inspect the body', leaving me with Douglas.

The Nookienomicon

"I had to push two slabs together," he explained. "She's quite…sizeable."

"Yes," was all I could say. I remembered her ducking through doorways in the dormitories and lifting the unruly out of their beds with one hand. She had been, by all accounts, a larger-than-life figure. "Have her family paid their respects?"

"No family. Far as I'm aware, she's in the hands of the State. Well, she'll be in the hands of the State soon enough. For now, she's in the hands of your little assistant."

"Annabelle is a professional."

"I can tell. But a professional what, that's the question."

I joined Annabelle downstairs as soon as I could muster the fortitude. She'd often taken the lead in the past while I settled accounts with Douglas. She insisted that she was quite at home downstairs and didn't need any help. On this occasion, I couldn't readily account for her eagerness.

When I entered the room, she dropped the sheet from her inspection of the body like I'd caught her stealing from a purse. She was flushed—I assumed it was the exertion of the stairs—and breathing a little more heavily than normal.

"You weren't kidding," Annabelle said.

"Is everything present and correct?"

"Amply so. Do you think she'll be happy to see us? It was always easy to tell with the other patients, but…"

"We are going to save her from the blackness of death's embrace. I am sure she will be thankful."

"I suppose we'd better hope so. She seems like

The Nookienomicon

she'd be a handful if she was angry. Several handfuls actually."

We prepared for the ritual as we had done every time before. Emboldened by success, I realised I'd left my protection in the car. Wholly irresponsible, but impatience was driving us now. I should have realised, like any man who proceeds unprotected, that this was folly and we would suffer for our haste.

Candles and chalk markings, incantations and more of the mysterious 'energy' that Annabelle always seemed to produce in such volume from the boarding house—they must have been so lively, the people there—and before I knew it, I saw the first stirrings of life beneath the sheet.

"Hellooo, Matron," Annabelle said.

Our patient rose, and once again the ill wind blew out our candles, but I had learned my lesson and shielded the lantern in every subsequent ritual. I watched the sheet fall away from a voluminous tangle of black hair and the most piercing, angry eyes I think I had ever seen.

And that was when I realised that Matron was most definitely *not* happy to see us.

Her hand snapped out and seized Annabelle by the throat. With inhuman strength, she lifted her off her feet. I caught a garbled string of syllables from my assistant that sounded almost like the words, "Choke me, Matron."

Casting around for something to use as a weapon, I found a conveniently placed axe in the corner. It was wholly inappropriate for Douglas to leave his chopper out in the mortuary, but on this

The Nookienomicon

occasion it might save a life.

I cleaved Matron's arm off at the elbow. Annabelle and the severed appendage flopped to the ground bonelessly. Matron flicked me the same foul look that usually presaged the words, 'You naughty boy', then slapped me into the wall with her other hand.

I collided with the table where I'd set the lantern and the flickering flame winked out. In the cold darkness that followed, I heard Matron sweeping across the room and stooping through the doorway. Upstairs, Douglas screamed again.

"Annabelle?" I asked, fumbling with the lantern. "Are you alright?"

"I'm fine," she muttered, sounding strained after her asphyxiation. "I might just…need some time alone, if that's okay."

"No time for that. We have to go after her."

"I mean, I absolutely agree, but it'd only take a minute."

"Annabelle, we can't delay. There's a one-armed giant woman on the loose and the good people of Arkham will be intimidated by her size and nudity."

"She can intimidate me any day."

The lantern returned to life—I am the Reanimator, after all—and revealed Annabelle, sprawled and panting on the floor beside Matron's sheet. Her arm was crawling across the stone towards the door, dragging itself with its fingers. Annabelle picked it up and stuffed it into the duffel where she kept her ritual supplies.

"For later," she said.

"Good idea. Perhaps we can use it to find

The Nookienomicon

Matron."

"Hey, that's thinking! I hadn't even considered that."

"Then why did you...? Never mind. There's no time to lose!"

***

Douglas was inconsolable, which was fortunate because we didn't have time to console him anyway. Matron's path of destruction was easy to follow. She'd ripped the mortuary door off its hinges, pulled down the fence and marched east, towards some unearthly beacon I couldn't fathom, shoving aside barriers as she went.

"You never told me she was so...forceful," Annabelle said, breathless from running, I presumed.

"Death has done nothing to mellow her, it seems."

"I wasn't complaining."

She had no spouse or lover of which I knew. The other bodies we had reanimated had returned to their homes and widows, so joyful at their reunion that they would spend all night and most of the next day in quiet seclusion. Annabelle insisted that it wasn't always quiet, but I elected not to pry.

Where Matron was going, I could not guess.

Until we turned a familiar corner, and I realised that we were in the Red Light District.

"Why would she come here?" I wondered aloud.

"Why *wouldn't* you come here?" Annabelle asked.

The Nookienomicon

"I suppose you're right. Everyone is very friendly."

Past a slew of stunned onlookers, who pointed us in the direction that our errant giantess had gone, we finally came to the front steps of the Silver Moonlight Lounge.

"Hmm, now that is strange," Annabelle muttered.

"What's that?"

"Well, I mean, there are probably a lot of places in the neighbourhood that'd be interested in a giant, naked woman, but this isn't one of them."

"Why not? She would make a very interesting specimen for a student of the arcane."

"No doubt, and I'd happily study her all week, but she doesn't have…the right equipment for the men here."

"You mean, she doesn't have arcane tomes and objects of power?"

Annabelle nodded. "Yes, one specific object of power these gentlemen are particularly interested in, if you know what I mean."

I didn't, but we'd already delayed too long. There was no one guarding the front stairs this time, so I burst into the building with Annabelle on my heels.

In the foyer, a group of men were tending to someone who'd been knocked to the ground. By Matron, I assumed.

"What happened here?" I demanded.

"An obscenely tall woman forced her way in and tried to march straight to Doctor Brunton's office. Of course, nobody tried to stop her, but Robert

The Nookienomicon

Pickman kept at her to pose for him. He does life drawing, you see, and a one-armed, grey-skinned gargantuan would have been right up his alley."

"Life drawing?" Annabelle asked. "That'd be tough, considering."

"Wait, did you say Robert Pickman?" I interjected. "Isn't he Upton as well?"

"Not all the time."

"Yes, I suppose that would get quite tiring, wouldn't it? So, where is the woman now?"

"We heard screaming coming from Doctor Brunton's office, so we assume she's in there."

"And nobody went to investigate?"

"Well, it's not unusual to hear screaming coming from Brunton's office, if I'm being honest. It's more polite just to wait."

"Quickly, Annabelle!"

I departed the scene in the foyer, and once again penetrated into the secret depths of the Silver Moonlight Lounge. At the sight of the giant Matron, the members had retreated, and probably wouldn't stir again until she had departed. In my haste, I hadn't actually worked out what, if anything, I could do about her.

As we neared Brunton's office, we were shocked by the sounds of screaming and a loud, rhythmic thumping. Annabelle, once again red with exertion, pulled a face that put me in mind of the Nookienomicon. Without pause, I shoved the doors open.

Brunton was cowering at the top of the ladder bolted to his bookshelves, and was hurling weighty tomes of forgotten lore at Matron's head. She

The Nookienomicon

swatted them aside with her remaining hand like they were nothing but flies. She was still just as intimidating as she'd been at the mortuary.

"Samuel Brunton, you come down here this instant," Matron demanded.

"You can't talk to me like that! I'm the Chairman of the Silver Moonlight Lounge!"

"You're not the Chairman of the Silver Moonlight Lounge; you're a very naughty boy. You placed the secrets of the Nookienomicon into the hands of the uninitiated and it could have spelled disaster. You're just lucky the two nitwits have only been resurrecting the husbands of randy housewives, or you might have caused the apocalypse."

"It's not my fault!" Doctor Brunton said, all of his earlier presence diminished. "The Nookienomicon demands to be used."

"You're a grown man, Samuel. You can't blame it on your tool. As an adult, you have to make rational decisions. And it means you have to be punished for your wrongdoings."

"Wait!" Annabelle yelled, pulling the Nookienomicon from her bag and brandishing it at Matron. "I'm the one who gathered the energy. I'm the one who spoke the incantation. I *demand* that you punish me instead. It's only right and proper."

Matron shook her head. "I couldn't possibly."

"Please?"

The giantess sighed, anger abating. She placed her remaining hand on Annabelle's head, and their size disparity became more obvious than ever.

"I might be willing to show mercy, on the

The Nookienomicon

provision that you commit to one final ritual. A circle of protection around Arkham, to prevent any evil that might come from your inexpert actions."

Annabelle nodded. "Well, if there's one thing I've learned through all this, it's that protection is important."

"We will need privacy," Matron said, "and an extremely large pool of...energy."

"I know a place we can go! It's downtown."

I got the impression that Annabelle was not affording the dangerous ritual the seriousness that it required. The poor girl was far too eager to atone for our sins, I was worried it had blinded her to the true nature of what Matron was proposing.

"I will also need my hand back," Matron said. "For the ritual."

"I was hoping you'd say that."

With that, they walked out of the office together, side-by-side. The last I saw of Annabelle Mater was the flash of a grin. The last I saw of Matron was everything.

***

And so, Annabelle and the Nookienomicon passed out of my life once and for all. I never heard from her, or Matron, again. The secrets of reanimation were also lost to me, and I tried to take solace in the fact that I had gone further in my study of death and rebirth than anyone before me.

The Silver Moonlight Lounge barred me for life. I would never again interfere with the members there. The women of the Red Light District

The Nookienomicon

consoled me, though they often seemed confused that I 'only wanted to talk'. After several months, I decided to take a sabbatical in Innsmouth, because surely it would be safer than Arkham.

Something about Annabelle, however, troubled me even after her disappearance. After thinking on it for quite some time, I must now share my apprehensions with you, gentle reader.

For all the time that I knew her, I fear, my sweet, gentle assistant may have in fact *been a lesbian.*

III

The Zann Sextet
By Chris Hewitt

"It's stiff. So, make sure you push it right in."

Hans bent over, blushing. "I say."

"Now, give the knob a good tug and a quick twist."

Blandot shoved his shoulder hard against the stubborn door. Once, twice, and the door flew open with a crack, sending the man stumbling into the dusty attic room. "See! Nothing a bit of elbow grease won't fix."

He retrieved the key from the rusty lock and handed it to his unimpressed new tenant.

Hans stared down his long nose at the boozy landlord, the funk of cheap wine and cheaper cigarettes turning his tee-total stomach. A shuttered window at the far end of the attic offered the only light, filtered through a forest of cobwebs. Amongst the spider's gossamer tapestry, he could make out a rusty metal bedstead, washstand, bookcase, and table, flanked by three rickety chairs.

"This can't have been my brother's room," said Hans, stepping over a desiccated rodent. "No one's lived here for an age."

"I can assure you these are your brother's lodgings. I guess he got behind on his dusting."

Hans wrinkled his nose as he brushed aside the cobwebs only for the sticky strands to cling to his frantically waving fingers. The dreary room seemed

The Nookienomicon

a squalid end for his brother. "They hailed my brother a Bratschenvirtuose back in Deutschland."

"Easy for you to say."

"No one played the viola like Erich. He was the darling of countesses from Titz to Wankendorf."

Blandot raised an eyebrow. "No wonder the fella needed a break."

"Indeed. What?" said Hans, uncertain if the Frenchman had understood him. "Where are the rest of my brother's belongings?"

Blandot's tongue flicked across his wine-stained lips. "Ah, about those. Your brother ran up sizeable arrears and he never mentioned any family, so... I sold them."

"Sold them! What about his viola?"

"Four francs at the pawnshop."

"Four francs! It's a priceless Stradivarius, owned by Lord Byron's granddaughter."

"I guess she must have dropped it."

Hans stared at the buffoon, mouth agape.

"Rent is four hundred francs a month," said Bardot, floorboards creaking as he picked his way through the filigree of filaments to the window.

"Four hundred!?"

"I know. I'm mad to ask so little for a prestigious location on the Rue d'Auseil. But I liked your brother. He never gave me any bother, kept himself to himself."

Bardot wrenched open the shutters, letting in the sepia daylight and awaking several irate bats that made a panicked flapping exit. He gagged, clutching a handkerchief to his face to mask the putrid stench wafting from the oily, dark river

The Nookienomicon

below. The open sewer snaked its way through the neighbourhood, carrying the diabolic detritus of countless Parisian households. "Three hundred and I'll have the address of that pawnshop."

Bardot looked set to haggle until Hans produced the cash.

"Fine. Fine. It'll be three months up front."

Hans flared his nostrils but counted out the money as Bardot scribbled a receipt.

"And tax. We run a legitimate business here."

Hans handed over the last of his money, wondering about the legitimacy of the bawdy brothel he'd passed on the first floor.

"Marvellous, Mr Zann," said Bardot, counting the money.

Hans stood tall, chest puffed out as he took the receipt. "The name is Jhobb. Erich was my half-brother. I'm a composer of some repute in Deutschland. Hans Jhobb. You've no doubt heard of me?"

Blandot furrowed his brow. "I'm not really into Bavarian oompah."

"Oompah? Oompah!"

"Stick it up yer jumper. That one of yours?"

"What? No! I'm a classical composer."

"Shame, I like that one. Anyway, I'm sure you're eager to settle in, try to keep the noise down. There's a good fella."

Blandot scuttled to the door, tongue slipping back and forth like a thirsty lizard. "Adieu, Monsieur Zann."

"It's Jhobb," Hans shouted out after the rapidly vanishing landlord. He moved to close the door,

57

The Nookienomicon

only to find it jammed with a pink shoe. The door swung open to reveal a rotund middle-aged lady, dressed in a pink burlesque outfit, her hand held out. "Patrice Pumpemour at your service. I understand we're to be neighbours?"

"News travels fast," mumbled Hans, limply shaking the woman's hand. "A pleasure, I'm sure. I'm Hans. Hans Jhobb."

Patrice raised her eyebrows. "Charmed, I'm so glad to have a gentleman for a neighbour. The last tenant proved to be an uncouth lout. Never said a word, just played his flipping fiddle every night and, oh, you've never heard such a racket. It came as no surprise, when, you know, they found him."

She stuck out her tongue and crossed her eyes, hand tugging at an imaginary noose.

"So, you knew my brother?"

Madame Pumpemour blanched and uncrossed her eyes. "Your brother?"

"Yes, Erich was my half-brother."

"Oh… I'm so sorry. Please accept my condolences."

"Yes, of course. Now, if you'll allow me to—"

"Of course, of course. If there's anything you need. I'm right across the hall. Anything, mind you."

Hans pushed the door to, his inane grin vanishing as it clicked shut.

"Fiddle player!" he hissed. The outlandish burlesque costume screamed of the woman's lack of taste. How far had his brother fallen to have to share a building with such people? It made no sense. The last letter Erich sent, he'd been gushing about his

The Nookienomicon

magnum opus, a piece of music so divine as to serenade the Gods.

Hans looked at the scribbled address on the crumpled receipt.

"Where did you leave it, Erich? Where is your masterpiece?"

***

Hans spent the week making the ramshackle apartment habitable and searching for any clues to his brother's work, all the while avoiding his nosy neighbour. Not a day passed without Madame Pumpemour darkening his door.

Blandot hadn't sold all his brothers' effects and amongst the cobwebs, Hans discovered several scraps of paper written in his brother's unintelligible hand. Then there was the handful of books, any expectations of musical theory replaced by more esoteric tomes. Had Erich found inspiration in the arcane works? Some secret buried in the pages of the Nookienomicon with its indecipherable texts and depraved drawings?

That had left only his brother's most valued belonging, his prized viola. It wasn't hard to find the pawnshop, tucked just off the Rue d'Auseil, lost amongst a bazaar of similar low-rent stores. It seemed the narrow dark alleyways with their leaning buildings lent themselves to a particular character of vendor.

The tinkle of a bell echoed around the dreary shop as Hans took in the eclectic objet d'art littering every surface. He could determine no order to the

The Nookienomicon

arrangement of wares. Rather, it seemed some ancient high tide had deposited the items higgledy-piggledy about the cramped space.

"Can I help you?" said a sullen old man, not looking up from his newspaper.

"Yes. I believe you can. I'm in the market for a viola."

The man gestured at his goods. "Does it look like I sell flowers?"

"Flowers?"

"If you want violas, try the Marché aux Fleurs. They'll rob you blind, mind you."

Hans' strong Bavarian accent had created several confusions since his arrival in France. His luggage being a case in point. He was sure it'd turn up at some point. But in this instance, it seemed the old man might be half deaf. "Oh, no. I'm after a viola. A good vioollaaa."

"Why didn't you say? Now that's something I can help you with. I was going to keep this one for myself, but I'm prepared to entertain a fair price."

The old man laid down his paper and rifled under the counter, retrieving a small package. Confused, Hans leaned forward and, teasing back the brown wrapping paper, he revealed a mottled blue-green wedge. A frightful stench stole his breath. "Ooh. What's that?"

The man looked at him, a mask of incredulity. "Gorgonzola! What you asked for. I was saving it for my lunch, but—"

"You fool. I don't want cheese or bloomin' flowers. I'm looking for a maple viola."

He performed a mocking fiddling action to

The Nookienomicon

emphasise his point.

The shopkeeper wrapped up his cheese, mumbling under his breath. "Your loss. Look, I'm a busy man. I don't have time to be messed about. But you're in luck. One came in only last week."

The man vanished out back and Hans cringed at the cacophony of bangs and crashes as if an orchestra had fallen down a flight of stairs. When the shopkeeper returned, he carried a stringed instrument tucked under his arm and Hans' heart leapt. "It will need restringing. But other than that, it's a quality piece."

"Ahh, now that's more like it," said Hans, all smiles as he took the instrument. A heartbeat later, his grin vanished, the instrument falling from his hand like he'd been burnt. "What's this monstrosity?"

"A mandola," said the shopkeeper, caressing the instrument's neck. "Do you know how rare they are these days? I get instruments in all the time, violins, violas, but never a quality mandola."

Hans leaned forward and shouted. "You deaf fool. I want a V-I-O-L-A. Not a MAND-ola. Not flowers, cheese or whatever this abomination is. I want a VI-ola."

He formed a V with the fingers of his left hand, adding an I with the middle finger of his right hand before gesticulating the digits in the shopkeeper's face. The man's lip curled into a snarl as he reached under the counter to retrieve a hefty oak table leg. The reddish-brown stain at its tip suggested it had seen plenty of use.

"Oh dear," said Hans, realising his mistake and

The Nookienomicon

hiding his hands behind his back. "I'm sorry. I think there's been a misunderstanding."

The shopkeeper poked the table leg into Hans' chest, marching him backwards out of the store. Hans stumbled on the uneven cobbles, still apologising as the old man spat a thick garlicky loogie in his face.

"No one insults a Frenchman or his cheese. If I see you around here again…"

He let the table leg punctate the threat before retreating into the store and turning the open sign to read out to lunch.

"I only wanted a viola."

A passer-by helped Hans to his feet. "If it's violas you want. You want to get along to the Marché aux Fleurs. Mind you, they'll—"

"Yes, I know, rob me blind," said Hans, straightening his collar and marching off up the alley.

***

Two nights later, Hans broke into the pawnshop, serenaded by a clowder of caterwauling cats. By moonlight, the Rue d'Auseil's squalid backstreets took on an altogether menacing atmosphere, the impenetrable shadows swallowing streetlights and his feeble flashlight.

A brick proved no match for a pane in the pawnshop door, and unlatching the lock, Hans crept inside. He'd half expected to find the shopkeeper asleep, leant back in his chair, snoring. But the store appeared empty as he tip-toed out back to where the

The Nookienomicon

shopkeeper kept his valuables. The flickering flashlight revealed a room twice the size and twice the disarray of the storefront. How the shopkeeper found anything amongst the chaos confounded Hans as he weaved his way through the bric-à-brac. It seemed people would pawn any and everything in the Rue d'Auseil.

Hans tripped and steadied himself by grasping at a well-endowed marble bust, almost toppling it from its plinth.

"Phoar. I mean, excuse me," he blurted, dropping his flashlight. The light rattled across the floorboards before flickering out. Hans held his breath, eyes adjusting to the gloom and to a dim light that shone from between the floorboards to cast long shadows onto the ceiling.

"Is-is there somebody there? Please, help me. What? No! I don't want to play."

Hans knelt and pressed his eye to a knothole in the well-worn board. A figure stood below him, the shopkeeper by the stench of blue cheese. He peered up at Hans, terrified eyes blinking with the falling dust. The old man had all the appearance of a busker, string instrument cradled in his left hand, bow in his right, and at his feet a carry case where a handful of coins glinted. The man argued with an unseen assailant and Hans feared someone else might have discovered the true value of his brother's viola.

"Please, God, help me," cried the shopkeeper, staring about the cellar, his eyes following some circling presence. "What? What do you mean which one? Azawhat? I don't understand. Your daemon

The Nookienomicon

sultan sounds lovely, but I'm not sure I want to meet him. No. Please don't. You can't make me. I won't—"

The shopkeeper screamed before doubling over in agony.

Hans strained to see the mysterious stranger, to hear the other side of the conversation, but he could hear no other words, see no other figures. He'd suspected the man might be a loon. Now he was in no doubt.

"No! I can't. I won't play."

A coin dropped from nowhere into the case, spinning for a moment before falling flat. The old man let out a gargled scream, jerking the viola to his shoulder. "Please."

Hans gasped as the crazed fool raised his brother's legendary instrument, a masterpiece of crafted maple. The shopkeeper bowed a long wavering note that made Hans' hair bristle as the darkness shifted and every shadow found new skittering legs, animated by the viola's perfect harmonics. When the note ended, the sound echoed for an eternity until Hans heard…

Miaow.

The cat slid past, hugging the shadows, and it was not alone. Others leapt and weaved their way in pursuit of the siren call that summoned them. An army of felines slinked past Hans before he plucked up the courage to peek through the knothole and what he saw turned his blood to ice. The cats surrounded the shopkeeper, an eager audience, licking their lips and sharpening their claws. They waited.

The Nookienomicon

"N-ni-nice pussies," cried the shopkeeper, cats weaving between his trembling legs. "Please don't make me. I didn't understand. I didn't, but now I do."

Another coin landed in the open case and the man's arm jerked, jamming the viola into his shoulder as the trembling bow inched towards the strings. The next note ripped the shop asunder, a whirlwind of tooth and claw. An infernal feline funnel, surrounded by the tumbling contents of the pawnshop as if a tornado had touched down in the basement. Hans ducked to avoid the crockery, gorgonzola and twirling buxom bust. The floorboards undulated and cracked before giving way as Hans leapt for the doorway. He missed, tumbling into the abyssal basement.

He came to, flashlight spinning beside him, illuminating the empty cellar. There was no sign of the shopkeeper, the mysterious assailant, or the feline army. The contents of the shop had vanished along with their owner. The only suggestion of a cataclysm, a persistent fur ball at the back of Hans' throat. Only the black leather viola case remained, laying on the floor beside Hans, and to his amazement, his brother's viola lay undamaged inside. He ran his finger along the embossed gold initials on the side of the case. *E. Z.*

"Oh, Erich, what have you done?"

***

Three sleepless nights later, Hans plucked up the courage to retrieve the viola from under a loose

The Nookienomicon

floorboard in his attic room. He'd fully expected the gendarme to burst through the door at any moment. But they never came, and he'd begun to doubt the whole crazy ordeal at the pawnshop had even happened. Sat at the table, he opened the viola case and ran his fingers over the magnificent instrument, remembering the endless hours his brother practised under their father's stern gaze.

"Where did you hide it, Erich?"

Hans turned his attention to the case, a handful of change clattering onto the table as he turned it over, and the shopkeeper's screams flooded back to him.

Knock. Knock.

Hans jumped, heart pounding as he stared at the door. "Who... who is it?"

Knock. Knock.

He rushed across the room and placed his ear to the door. "The knocking shop is downstairs. *Downstairs!*"

Knock. Knock.

Hans rolled his eyes and flung open the door, only to be drowned in a tidal wave of chiffon as Madame Pumpemour shot past, a bottle of wine under her arm and another on her breath.

"I don't make a habit of visiting a gentleman's room in the dead of night."

She staggered to the table, producing two glasses from the folds of her bustle and filled each to the brim.

"Madame Pumpemour—"

She held up her hands. "Please, call me Patrice. I insist."

"I'm in the middle of—"

The Nookienomicon

She necked one of the glasses. "Today is my birthday. Did you know that? Of course not. No one remembered. No one cares."

"I'm sorry, but I really don't have time for this."

She flopped into a chair, tears flooding down her powdered cheeks as she started on the second glass.

"There was a time they held a ball on my birthday. I wasn't always a burlesque singer, you see. Once I was a celebrated soprano. The toast of Paris. A voice to die for. That's what the critics said."

Hans sighed, rubbing his forehead. "Yes. Yes. I'm sure they did."

Patrice emptied the second glass. "Back then my voice was pure, powerful enough to fill the Palais Garnier."

Hans crossed his arms. "Pure nonsense more like."

Patrice's face became a scowling thunderstorm as she shot somewhat precariously to her feet. Anticipating her departure, Hans held open the door. Instead, Patrice held up an empty glass and took a deep quivering breath before unleashing a banshee's screech. The noise rattled Hans' teeth, shattering the windows and exploding the wine bottle. He covered his ears, cowering as the wine glasses followed and Patrice collapsed into the chair, hiccupping and pulling splinters of glass from her hair. "I've still got it. But who wants an ageing opera singer?"

Hans stared gobsmacked at the shards strewn about his room, the table, his brother's viola. "What have you done?"

The Nookienomicon

"What haven't I done? I could tell you some tales."

"Oh, I say," blushed Hans.

"No, not like that. Cheeky. Although I am lucky if I get a club booking these days."

"I'm not surprised. You'd put them out of business."

"Oh," said Patrice, swaying as she took in her handiwork, brushing the glass from the viola. The instrument rattled as she picked it up.

Hans froze, mortified as Patrice turned the viola over and, holding it by the fingerboard, shook the instrument before banging the body.

"Oh, what's this? There's something poking out of your f-hole."

"My f'ing what?"

"Your f'ing-hole, look it's jammed right in there."

Patrice teased a page from the viola's swirling sound hole before tossing the instrument to Hans, who caught it haphazardly with both hands.

She unfolded the paper, turning it one way, then the next as she scrutinised its contents. "It's full of doodles."

Hans plucked the note from her grasp, his fingers dancing over the inane scribblings. "It's my brother's hand."

"I wonder why he stuffed it in his f-hole."

"Indeed," mumbled Hans, his mind elsewhere. He'd seen similar pictographs within the pages of the Nookienomicon.

"It's a code. That must be it," he cried, retrieving his brother's notes, feet crunching on broken glass.

The Nookienomicon

He laid the fragments around the new page, arranging and re-arranging the pieces until they fit into a mystic jigsaw that shimmered for a moment.

Patrice picked up what remained of the wine bottle and sighed. "I do love a good jigsaw, but it's so annoying when they're missing a piece."

"It's not a jigsaw. It's a musical score. Erich's final composition."

Hans could hear the music in his head, a discordant symphony, and amongst the chaos of notes and jarring beats ran a dark underlying genius. "It's magnificent."

"If you say so. It looks like gibberish to me."

"Yes. Don't you see? Erich tried to play it by himself, and it drove him mad."

"Well, that explains the terrible noise he'd make."

Hans tried to separate the parts out, the effort making his head spin. "It would take half a dozen people to play this. A sextet."

"Oh Hans, kinky. But you know what they say. When in Paris… I'll go and ask if anyone is interested downstairs."

"No, not strumpets. Trumpets. Musicians."

"Musicians?"

"Yes. To have any chance of performing Erich's masterpiece, we'll need at least a flutist, cellist, percussionist and hornist…"

Hans wandered off, lost in thought as he deconstructed the song buzzing around his head like a trapped bee.

Patrice looked at him. "Horniest what?"

"What? No, horn-ist, a horn-ist, you know

The Nookienomicon

someone who plays the French horn."

"I can still go downstairs. It sounds right up their alley."

"Never mind. We'll also need to find a vocalist and violist. Now, I can play Erich's viola, not as well as my brother, but good enough."

"And you have your vocalist."

"I do?" said Hans, realising his mistake as Patrice crossed her arms and stared at him with daggers. "Oh yes, of course. Wonderful. Two down."

Patrice sprang to her feet and hugged him, planting a big red kiss on his lips. "It's sorted then. I'll reach out to some of my old contacts and get the message out. We'll assemble your sextet. The Zann Sextet, in memory of your brother."

"Yes. I like the sound of that."

Patrice danced to the door. "Thank you, Hans. This is the best birthday present ever."

She closed the door and Hans slumped into the chair, his mind racing with Erich's haunting music. He'd have his work cut out, transposing his brother's scribblings, but if it didn't drive him to madness, then the world would hear Erich's swan song. "The Zann Sextet. Yes, I think Erich would like that."

***

"It's gone seven. Where are they?" asked Hans, pacing the attic room.

Patrice had been practising her scales for half an hour, setting his nerves and remaining crockery on

The Nookienomicon

edge.

"You know how tricky it can be to find the Rue d'Auseil. They're probably lost."

Knock. Knock.

"See. Here they are."

Hans flung open the door and bowed. "Good evening, Hans Jhobb and you are?"

"Hans Jhobb?"

The stranger glanced left and right before stepping in and handing Hans his dirty mac. "Bit forward. Change of management?"

"Yes. I've taken over my brother's lodgings."

"Good. Good. So, is this all you got?"

"Sorry? What?"

The stranger nodded to Madame Pumpemour. "I mean any port in a storm and all that. But if I'm paying top franc, I was hoping for something a little more... well... sporty."

Patrice sauntered over to the man. "Sporty, is it? I'll give you bloody sporty."

True to her word, she delivered a kick to the man's nether regions that made Hans squeal and the stranger drop to the floor whimpering.

"The Rumpy Pumpy Palace is downstairs, pervert!"

The man staggered to his feet, snatching back his mac as he stuffed twenty francs in Hans' jacket pocket. "Sorry, mate. I'm not into the rough stuff."

"I haven't even started," hissed Patrice.

The bowlegged man fled crab-like, and Hans closed the door behind him.

"The cheek of it. I'll have a word with his wife tomorrow. Then he'll get what for."

The Nookienomicon

"You know him?"

Patrice spat. "Bloody politicians."

Knock. Knock. Knock.

"What now?" whined Hans, opening the door.

A middle-aged man removed his beret.

"Hi, I'm Jack. I'm the hornist."

"Downstairs!" cried Hans, slamming the door closed.

"No, that's the hornist," cried Patrice.

"Yes, I heard him, filthy beast."

"No, he's the horn player."

She rushed over and flung open the door. "I'm so sorry. Jack, is it?"

"Yes, Jack Horner," said Jack, holding up the case with his French horn.

"Marvellous, if you'd like to set up in the corner. We're expecting the rest of the group any moment."

"Great. I'll get my slides greased up and be right with you."

Hans flared his nostril and whispered to Patrice. "Are you sure he's our man?"

A loud thud announced Blandot heaving a monstrous black chest up the flight of stairs, followed by a voluptuous young lady, her blouse doing more heavy lifting than her red-faced sherpa. "Thank you, Mr Blandot. It's so kind of you to help me. I'd never have got it up by myself."

Blandot lifted the enormous case onto the landing. The only work Hans had seen the man do. He'd certainly made himself scarce when Hans had been moving in.

"You're welcome. Maybe I can help you go down later?"

The Nookienomicon

"Cheeky," grinned the woman, turning her attention to Hans.

"Ah, you must be Hans. It's nice to meet you. I'm Norma Stitz, the cellist."

"More like a double bass, if you ask me," cackled Blandot.

"Oh, Mr Blandot."

"Indeed," said Hans, almost tripping over himself to help her with her huge load. Patrice barged him aside before he could get his hands on her enormous chest. "Norma, glad you could join us. If you could set up next to Jack Horner in the corner. We're just waiting for a few more."

Blandot helped wheel Norma's Cello inside before making his excuses.

"Looks like you're planning quite a party, Hans."

"Yes. We're putting together a sextet."

"Well, I'll tell you what I tell them downstairs. Twenty percent, no questions asked," said Blandot, tapping his nose.

"No! Not a sex shop. A sextet, six musicians."

"I know you arty types. One minute it's Brahms and Listz, the next it's all Tietz and Foucquet. All I'm saying is, if there's any fiddling going on, I want my share. In the meantime, keep the noise down. I don't want you upsetting the other tenants."

A whip-crack and a scream echoed up the stairwell.

"Looks like someone forgot the safety word again," said Blandot, rolling his eyes and setting off down the stairs. He met a stranger halfway down, and they shuffled back and forth. "Better rates and a better time downstairs, fella."

The Nookienomicon

"Better rates?" asked the stranger, but Blandot was gone.

"Cooee," called Patrice, waving at the figure. "Are you here for the sextet?"

The man climbed the stairs, white stick flicking back and forth as he felt his way along the banister. "Yes. Yes. The names Chap Lipz. Are you Patrice? Larry sends his regards."

"I ain't seen Larry in years."

"That makes two of you," interjected Hans, waving his hand in front of the man's sunglasses.

"Is he still editing that old Jazz Mag?"

"You know Larry. Never happier than when he's blowing his own trumpet. He told me you needed a flutist."

"Well, yes. Ideally, one who can read music," said Hans.

Patrice waved at him to be quiet.

"Ah, you've noticed then. Don't worry it's not a problem. Bonnie, here, can read, can't you girl."

Hans looked about, finding only a dangling length of cord hanging from Chap's hand. "Erm?"

Chap felt around by his side. "God damn it, girl! She's always wandering off. Bonnie!"

"Alright already. I'm coming," yelled a teenage girl, stomping her way up the stairs to take Chap's hand.

"As I was saying, my niece can read and translate for me."

Bonnie scowled at Hans, chewing bubble gum and punctuating her uncle's words with a loud pop.

"I'm sure it'll be fine," said Patrice, ushering Chap and Bonnie inside and introducing them to the

The Nookienomicon

rest of the group.

Hans turned to close the door, but a cacophony of bangs and crashes echoed up the stairwell. "What now? A one-handed pianist?"

The noise grew louder as a monstrous figure climbed the stairs, to the beat of a drum and a crash of a cymbal. The one-man shambles came to a halt at the top of the stairs, gasping, catching his breath.

"And who, pray tell, are you?" asked Hans.

"Lee Vitout."

Hans' jaw dropped. "No reason to be rude. It was only a question."

"No… my… name… is… Lee… Lee Vitout. Lance said you needed a whey, hey, hup, percussionist," said the stranger, a cacophony of bangs and clanks ending with a penny whistle as the man twitched and spasmed.

Patrice arrived a moment later. "Ah, our last member… and your name is?"

"Lee Vitout," said Hans.

"It was only a question."

"That's what I said."

"It's my, hip, hip, whup name," implored Lee, trembling knees clanging a pair of cymbals together. "I'm… I'm… I'm…."

"Very welcome," said Patrice taking his hand and guiding the rattling one-man-band inside.

Hans closed the door and surveyed his ragtag sextet, shaking his head. He needed skilled musicians but instead Patrice had rounded up a bunch of vagrants who'd be lucky to aspire to be buskers.

The Nookienomicon

***

"Okay, settle down. Settle down," yelled Hans, failing to get the attention of the group. Patrice cleared her throat, and the room fell quiet, all but for the pop of Bonnie's bubble gum.

"Thank you. My name is Hans Jhobb. You're no doubt familiar with my handiwork."

The sextet sniggered.

"Been a while," said Lee, accompanied by a sliding tin whistle.

"Only two francs downstairs," said Jack.

Lee checked his pockets.

"What? Never mind," said Hans, shaking his head. It seemed Parisians were always getting the wrong end of the stick. "I am a composer of some note in Deutschland."

The sextet exchanged blank looks. Pop.

"Never mind. My brother, Erich Zann—"

"The violist?" asked Jack Horner.

"You knew my brother?"

"Sure, everyone knew Erich the Earworm."

"Earworm?"

"Yeah, that was Erich's nickname on the Jazz scene, on account of his tunes worming their way into your head," said Chap, head snaking back and forth.

Norma shuffled uncomfortably. "What was that track he'd end with at The Blue Pearl? Nuclear… something."

"Chaos," offered Chap.

"Nuclear Chaos. Gives me goosebumps even now," said Norma, her ample bosom juggling back

The Nookienomicon

and forth long after the shiver ran up her spine. "I couldn't get it out of my head for a fortnight. Nearly drove me mad, it did."

Pop! "I heard he sold his soul to the devil."

"That's just superstitious nonsense, kid," said Jack.

Chap nodded. "You're probably right, but damn if he couldn't fiddle."

"Amen," barked Lee, his flailing hands failing to cover his mouth.

Hans handed out the hand-written translation of his brother's score.

"My late brother—"

Pop! "Told ya. The devil always collects what he's owed."

"—wrote one final score. His magnum opus, so to speak. I've taken his notes—"

"Scribblings more like," added Patrice

"—and fleshed them out. Tonight, with your help, I aim to make my brother's dream a reality, to make his music live again by performing Azathoth."

"Gesundheit," said Patrice.

"No. The piece is called Azathoth."

Pop! "Has a what?"

"Sense of humour. What kind of name is that?" said Norma.

"Look. Just learn the score, get set up and we'll do a rehearsal in half an hour."

***

It took an hour for the sextet to read their scores and tune their instruments. Any adherence to the

The Nookienomicon

diatonic scale, major or minor, fell by the wayside in pursuit of a new musical language. That was the genius Hans had seen in his brother's work, a discovery he could never have imagined. He tapped his bow on the table. "Are we ready?"

"As we'll ever be," said Chap. His niece had played the notes on the old man's fingers, several times, before she'd convinced him she'd not misread the score. "I mean, I like my free form Jazz, but this is far out."

"I grant you it's a bit experimental. But I'm sure Erich was heading somewhere with it."

Jack lifted his horn. "A padded cell would be my guess."

"Genius is often confused with madness."

"And madness with genius," mumbled Jack.

"Well, we'll never know unless we try," said Hans, nestling the viola into the nape of his neck and tapping a count.

The opening bars set the scene, long twisting viola chords. Notes that shouldn't go together but somehow, they worked. Norma joined in as Hans hit a refrain, the bass notes of her cello not remotely harmonising with the viola's pitch or measure. The notes tumbled over each other, flat and sharp, indistinguishable from each other, but in amongst the chaos Hans could sense a new order. A new kind of music. No, not new, ancient, primordial.

Jack's horn slid into the discord, a long blaring announcement of a change in tone, bringing a new depth, a new darkness. The sound resonated in the attic space, thrumming the air, amplifying the effect as the piece built. Chap's flute entered the fray next,

The Nookienomicon

dancing between the discordant elements hinting at purpose within the chaos as the tune took on a life of its own.

"Yes, that's it," yelled Hans, his bow a blur, fingers bleeding. He nodded to Patrice who hesitated. "Now, Patrice. Now."

She straightened her back, her face transforming into a mask of resolve as she took a long breath and sang. Incomprehensible words spilt from Patrice's larynx, mingling with the cacophony of chaos where her soprano voice bound the other elements into commands, instructions that shook the fabric of the building, words that railed at the natural order of things.

Bonnie held her hands over her ears, fear in her eyes as she pleaded with her uncle, to Patrice, to any of them to stop. Lost in a rapturous fervour they would not, could not hear her. Slipping the cord that bound her to her uncle, Bonnie ran, slipping and sliding across the shaking room and out the door.

"Is this your idea of keeping it down?" hollered Blandot, poking his head around the door. "Oi, Jhobb, you hear me. Turn it down."

Hans spun around, his feet no longer touching the floor as he frenetically fiddled. Eyes that only saw madness stared back at the landlord with profound indifference.

"Tell you what. Never mind. Forget I mentioned it," said Blandot, receding back down the stairwell as quick as his legs would carry him.

Only Lee remained, instrument held tight, barely suppressing his nervous twitching as he prepared to drop the beat. When the moment arrived, Lee struck

The Nookienomicon

his cowbell like an over-wound alarm clock, the tuneless clanking the final piece of the jigsaw as the attic room ceased to exist.

***

"Oh, bravo, bravo."

Hans' head swam as he stared up at a skinny bespeckled fop, waving a handkerchief in his face. He'd been to a few parties in his time, woken up under many a table, but never with what felt like a cleaver buried between his eyes. "What happened? Where I am?"

"I guess you could say you've made it to the after-party."

Hans groaned, staring at his shredded fingers. He could hear the rest of the sextet stirring somewhere behind him.

"What time is it?"

The stranger pulled out a pocket watch and tapped it. "Ah, well that's a bit of a moot question."

"Who are you again?"

"Oh, where are my manners? I'm Nembra, but my friends just call me Tru."

Hans sat up, the room swimming around him. "Tru Nembra? Have we met?"

"Oh, no. But I knew your brother."

Hans shook his head, instantly regretting the sudden motion. "Another free form jazz fan?"

"Indeed. Your brother's second biggest fan. My boss and your new benefactor being his biggest fan."

"Boss? Benefactor? What?"

The Nookienomicon

The room shook, a long bass groaning rumble that dislodged dust from the beams.

"Ah, talk of the devil. Look, you and your chums, take your time. I'll pop back just after I've found out what the blind idiot wants now. Okay?"

"What? No, wait!"

Tru vanished, jolting Hans from his stupor as he stared at the remains of the attic room. Half the ceiling was missing, replaced by a peculiar purple fog. He staggered to the window, to find The Rue d'Auseil gone, along with the toxic black river and for that matter the rest of Paris. The thick swirling mist enveloped the room.

Patrice slumped into a chair, her face hitting the table with a thump. "Never again. Two glasses of cheap plonk, and I'm wrecked. I'm getting too old for all-night parties."

"What party?" said Hans, memory flooding back to him. "Weren't we rehearsing?"

Patrice raised her head, hair clung to her face. "I was singing..."

Lee stirred with a crash of cymbals that solicited several groans, the loudest from Jack who awoke with a start, his hands grasping Norma's enormous... cello. "What the hell happened?"

"I don't know," said Hans, walking to the door and flinging it open to reveal the stairwell missing, replaced by the thick fog. "But I don't think we're in Paris anymore."

"Nonsense!" cried Jack, striding past to teeter on the edge of the abyss. "What on Earth?"

"Bonnie!" cried Chap, holding up the loose cord. "Where is she?"

The Nookienomicon

His hands scrambled around the floor, in search of his niece.

"She's not here," said Norma, comforting the old man.

"She got away. I saw her run, just before…"

Hans' voice trailed off as he recalled floating into the air, his body a marionette, the musical chords his strings.

"Hans, what's going on? I'm scared," begged Patrice.

"Yes, Hans. Spill the beans," said Tru, sitting at the window. A silver walking cane and top hat now complimented his absurd period costume.

"Who the hell are you?" cried Jack.

"Tru Nembra," said Hans, rushing across the room to pick up the Nookienomicon and flick through its dusty pages. "I knew I'd heard that name. It says here you're the angel of music."

"Guilty as charged," said Tru, bowing and tipping his hat.

"You don't look like an angel to me," said Patrice.

"I get that a lot. Do you think it's the lack of wings?"

"Where's my niece?" asked Chap.

Tru shrugged. "Your guess is as good as mine. She's not here, so I guess she's back where you came from."

"We're not in Paris?" cried Norma.

"Oh no, you're a long way from Paris. Welcome to the Final Void, the Court of the daemon sultan Azathoth. Supreme Lord and creator of all things, blind dreamer, lord of all, the deep dark, Him in the

The Nookienomicon

gulf, yadda, yadda, yadda. You get the idea."

The sextet stared at him blankly.

"The blind idiot god, Nuclear Chaos, the cold one?"

Still, not a flicker of recognition appeared on the groups' faces.

With a wave of his walking stick, the swirling mists above the room cleared and Tru pointed up. "Him."

Hans looked up into the face of Azathoth, into chaos incarnate and his mind cracked. With splintered nails, he clawed at his eyes, anything to not see the incompressible truth that slumbered above him. The group's tortured screams echoed in his ears, muted against his own uncontrollable banshee wailing.

"What's happening?" yelled Chap.

"Oh sorry, just a tick," said Tru, with another wave of his hand.

"I-I can see," cried Chap, removing his glasses, his face beaming until he followed the gaze of the others. "Oh, God. No! I can see."

Chap set to his new eyes with his flute, utter joy to unfathomable despair too far for any man to fall.

Tru restored the shroud of mist with a waggle of his walking stick and the group collapsed, whimpering and vomiting. Norma tugged the bloody flute from Chap's trembling fists. "It's okay. You've just got a little something in your eye."

She retrieved his discarded sunglasses, sliding them over the old man's bloody eyeless sockets. "There you go. All better."

The angel of music helped Hans into a chair.

The Nookienomicon

"I'm sorry. But I find words fail when it comes to old Az. Show, don't tell, isn't that what they say?"

"You're no angel," sobbed Patrice, scratches down her red cheeks.

"Now, don't be like that. I'm here to help."

"Help!" cried Lee, falling over himself. "I'll never be able to sl-sl-sleep again."

"Now you know how I feel. I've been responsible for keeping old Az here asleep for an eternity now. It's only my lulling symphony that's kept the idiot from waking and devouring your world for breakfast. So, in a way, you owe me."

"Owe you? All you're owed is a slap," said Jack.

"Look, I'll make this easy for you. I deserve a holiday and for the first time in forever I have an opportunity to work on my tan."

"You do look a bit pasty," said Patrice.

"I know. A millennium without sun will do that. That's why I need you, talented souls, to hold the fort while I recharge my batteries. Keep old grumpy draws asleep and your universe safe."

"Oh, screw this," said Jack heading for the door. "I want to go back. Send me back."

"Maybe I'm not making myself clear," said Tru, transforming into a striped red and white swimming costume, his handkerchief now a knotted hat, cane replaced by a bucket and spade. "I'm going on holiday. If you think the daemon sultan here is a little scary asleep, trust me, this is nothing compared to when he's awake. He's not much of a morning person."

Tru walked across the room. "Don't worry, it's just a holiday. A brief break in the sun and I'll be

The Nookienomicon

right back."

"When?" asked Hans.

"I don't know. A couple of centuries," said Tru, stepping through the door and vanishing into the mist, with nothing more than a cheeky wink. "Give or take."

"This is madness," cried Jack, following the angel of music out the door only to fall from sight. A second later came a wailing scream, followed by a crash, and he arrived unceremoniously back in the ruined attic room.

"Mind the step," he gasped, before passing out.

"A century? How long is that? Only, I got a hair appointment on Friday," asked Norma.

"I don't think you'll be making it," said Patrice.

Hans stared up into the mist. Is this what happened to his brother? Had Erich been nothing more than a long weekend for the mischievous angel of music? The shopkeeper a long lunch?

A deep rumbling threatened to shake the attic apart as the Blind Idiot God shifted in his sleep.

Hans picked up the viola and tapped. "One, two, three."

IV

Lady Chatterly's Blowhole
by Beth W. Patterson

"That fishy smell! I can't seem to be able to control it!" the young woman's voice wailed.

"Well, Fanny, you'll have to find yourself some sort of remedy by tonight," replied her husband. "It is our honeymoon, after all."

"No, Melvin, I mean the breeze coming in off the water!" Fanny stopped in her tracks, set down her suitcase, and gestured helplessly at the waterfront. "Why did we have to choose Innsmouth for our romantic getaway? There's nothing scenic about this harbour!"

'Nothing scenic' was quite the understatement. The rows of buildings lining the waterfront had fallen into disrepair with their broken windows and caved-in roofs. The only natural feature to gaze at was the forbidding long black line of Devil Reef.

"Because it was the cheapest location, and we're trying to save our resources. I'm trying to become a famous artist, remember?" He tilted the brim of his fedora, the better to gaze lovingly into her eyes. Tightening his coat around himself, he reached out to tuck a wisp of her auburn hair behind her ear. "That's why you fell for me in the first place."

Fanny sighed with a tiny squeak. "It's true. The name Mrs. Fanny Futterbuck has a ring to it, and I want the world to envy me once you spew forth your creations. That up-and-coming Jackson

The Nookienomicon

Pollock has nothing on you!"

Melvin threw his arms around her waist. "Then let's get things rolling," he purred in her ear. "We'll check into our hotel, play a game of 'hide the sausage', and you can be my creative muse!"

***

The beaming gap-toothed woman seemed out of place in the grim New England town. Her oversized pillbox hat sported an enormous star lined with esoteric-looking writing, as if snatched from a celebrity demon's dressing room door. Unlike the silent fish-eyed natives of Innsmouth, she greeted them with a nearly cloying warmth.

"Welcome to Gilman House!" she squealed. "I'm Lady Chatterly, the new owner of this establishment." She took their suitcases, then led them to a foyer. Taking a spot in an ornate-looking cathedra chair, she motioned for the couple to seat themselves on an adjacent couch.

"Goodness me, it's been so long since we've had any new visitors around these parts," she chirped. "Last time was when my daughter was still training to work in the gold refinery. She's got three children of her own, can you believe? And she also has this little dog, whom everyone says is quite the…"

Whatever the loquacious woman said next was a blur of completely irrelevant jabber. Neither husband nor wife knew quite how the soliloquy went, as they blindly fumbled for each other's hands, looking for a polite way to bid her good

The Nookienomicon

night and escape to their room.

"...but for someone to learn typing? When is that ever going to come in handy? That's just what my hairdresser said when I was there last. I suppose it was two weeks ago, or maybe three? I can never keep the lunar calendar straight these days, but my co-workers used to go on and on about it..."

Melvin's eyes glazed over. His wife slumped in her chair. Every valiant effort at being cordial was countered by the soporific effect of the proprietress's monologue. They daydreamed of unspeakable horrors beneath the waves, then snapped to attention and tried to smile politely.

"...just not right for the Esoteric Order of Dagon, and I told my husband, God rest his soul, that if he began to take on the appearance of the locals, it would have to mean that many years ago one of his ancestors crossed the captain..."

The vision of myriad hungry mouths snapped Melvin out of his hypnotic torpor. "Lady Chatterly, our deepest apologies, but we really must retire to our room at once!"

He pulled his nearly comatose wife to her feet and helped her up the stairs, more and more out of earshot. It took him several tries to insert his key. A quick jerk of his hand on the knob got the job done, the door swung open, and they were alone in their quarters at last.

***

Lying on the hard bed, Melvin could only grunt. Fanny was curious about this wondrous game her

The Nookienomicon

new husband had promised her, but something in Lady Chatterly's incessant prattle seemed to have affected the man's ability to keep his promises. Even Fanny had to admit that the nonstop chatter had been nearly traumatic to her senses. She couldn't even find a sausage in their luggage, and the sparse furnishings didn't seem to offer much in lieu of hiding places. The carpet didn't even match the drapes. So, she finally came to bed and snuggled against Melvin, taking in the strangeness of sharing a bed with another human being.

Hoping to take their minds off the flaccid trunk of the elephant in the room, the new bride piped up, "Have you ever encountered such a blabbermouth as our hostess? I don't know about you, but I never once saw her take a breath."

"Her mouth is certainly tireless," concurred Melvin. "It's as if that singular orifice serves no function except to rid the body of toxic waste."

Fanny let out a tight puff of amusement. "Do you mean…?"

"Carbon dioxide!" crowed her husband. "The process of exhalation. And quite frankly, I don't know how she can respire with that incessant chatter. Do you suppose she has an additional way to breathe?"

Mrs. Futterbuck's mouth puckered in concentration. "Like a dolphin's blowhole?"

Her groom paused in his surreptitious hand motions he'd sworn up and down had been arm curls. "You know something, dear? You may be onto something. Suppose she had an unusual deformity!" He patted her hand. "Perhaps it's

The Nookienomicon

hidden beneath that garish hat with the enormous star."

"Do you think you can penetrate it?" Fanny asked hopefully.

"The blowhole or the star?" yelped Melvin.

"The hat!" insisted his new wife. "We just need to remove it and plug up that extra hole. Lady Chatterly is clearly not of this world."

"Imagine if I could lay eyes upon such terrifying wonders," Melvin purred with sudden excitement. "The things I could paint! It would set the world on its ear, the likes of which would not have been seen since Hieronymus Bosch…"

As her husband's demeanour turned cheerful, Fanny realised that she was already worn out for the day. Eventually they both succumbed to slumber, resolved to consummate their marriage on the morrow.

***

The following morning proved to be just as frustrating. Fanny opened her eyes to see the most curious formation of the bedsheets, like a miniature pup tent. Her husband reached for her, drawing her close and kissing her throat, hands wandering her hips and thighs through her sheer dressing gown. As he rolled over and hoisted himself atop her, he began to murmur, "Oh, Fanny…Fanny…I could just eat you up." She gasped and began to undo the buttons of her nightdress, revealing her creamy…

A loud knock on the door made them both yelp. "Wakey, wakey! Eggs and bakey!" cried Lady

The Nookienomicon

Chatterly on the other side of the door.

"Perhaps it's time we had a romantic stroll through the town to see if we might find some sort of alternative lodging," growled Melvin

"And let's find a place to get some food away from that wretched woman," suggested his wife. "This Fanny is long overdue for a feeding!" They rolled out of bed and padded to their suitcases, trying to clothe themselves as quietly as possible.

The knocking continued for a moment, then the squish of something large and wet began to thump the door more insistently. It made Fanny's hair curl.

"If we find a way to make it onto the slate roof," hissed Melvin, "we can lower ourselves onto the street along the opposite end of the lobby."

"First see if you can even pry open that window," his wife whispered back.

The young man went to the sill and grunted. "It's really tight!" he complained.

"Push harder!" Fanny barked. She ran to help him, and the pair managed to lift it together.

Melvin assessed the size. "It's wide enough for my head to go through, so the rest of me should be no problem."

"Goodness, me, have I arrived at an inopportune time?" gurgled Lady Chatterly from the other side of the door. "If you think this is awkward, you should hear about the time I went into the Masonic Hall one April morning, forgetting that it was close to the time of year when all the young men tended to…"

The curtain rod didn't appear to be strong

The Nookienomicon

enough to support the weight of either adult, so Melvin looped the moth-eaten velour curtain over the edge of the iron bed frame. Crawling out of the window, he pulled the shabby drapery though and gave an experimental yank. The metal banged against the wall as Melvin tested the security. With a giant leap of faith, he swung to the ground, landing neatly on his feet.

The wet thumping at the door continued, and Fanny tried not to panic. "Oh, do be careful!" she called over to her new groom. "We've never tried anything like this before. I never thought we'd be swingers. Why did we have to go to such measures?"

"Well, we all have to make sacrifices!" was Lady Chatterly's unsolicited response. "As a matter of fact, our community is demanding some such, but I keep forgetting about it, with all of my pedicures. They keep getting the colour wrong! There's also this book club they hold every Tuesday at Miskatonic…"

"Mg ai!" growled the new bride, and the monologue paused. This bought her a moment to clear her head. Fanny was slicker than her husband and followed suit without a sound. It was hard for her to remain inconspicuous swinging on a curtain to the ground in broad daylight, but the streets appeared to be deserted.

Trying to appear as casual as any couple that had just escaped an upstairs window, the Futterbucks made their way quickly across town with no particular destination in mind.

The Nookienomicon

***

The long stroll through the town was anything but romantic. As they moved deeper into the heart of the residential area, the buildings seemed to have fallen into increasing amounts of disrepair. The old churches looked downright sinister.

Many of the locals had what was referred to as the "Innsmouth look", with large unblinking eyes, wide, frog-like mouths, and narrow heads. They seemed outright hostile, but it was still better than the auditory assault of Lady Chatterly's jabbering.

But when the newlyweds turned a corner, they encountered a new kind of Innsmouth denizens. Their heads were completely fishlike, unblinking eyes staring up at the trio. The shabby coats and trousers did little to conceal their ranine bodies and greyish-green skin.

Melvin Futterbuck could not resist pulling his sketchbook from his coat pocket. "What a vision," he crooned.

"Couldn't you be a bit more subtle?" protested Fanny. "I don't think they like being stared at, let alone being drawn. Why can't you carry a single page in case inspiration strikes?"

"It's a leatherbound sketchbook. The pages are sewn into it. So either I whip it out right now or tear one off."

One of them spoke in an intelligible croak. "Ahf' ymg' ah llll mgr'luh?"

"We're not looking at anything," replied Fanny tightly. She tugged at her husband's sleeve. "Darling, they appear to be getting hostile."

The Nookienomicon

"I'm not asking them to pose for me like French girls!" snapped Melvin.

"This is going to be worse than Lady Chatterly's blowhole…"

The monstrous men suddenly approached. "Mgshugnah!" burbled one, and they began to approach the couple, loping into a gait that was something between crawling and hopping.

The Futterbucks tried to shuffle away at as brisk a pace as they could manage. The patter of webbed feet and the unmistakable sounds of hopping behind them drew nearer.

The chase was on.

Running along any streets parallel to the Manuxet River seemed like a spectacularly bad idea. The pursuers appeared to be built for swimming, and there was no telling how many more might be hiding near their element.

"Look for a market…a shop…a fire station…" panted Melvin. "Any place…where people might help us…"

"They're gaining on us! Why don't we overturn a fruit cart?" wailed Fanny. "That's what they do in the movies!"

They turned a corner and found a dead end. The monstrous-looking creatures blocked their escape.

One wearing a gold circlet around his head and clad in long priestly robes—presumably their leader—made its way to the front of the throng. Flaring its gills, it opened its robe to expose itself and all that its infernal breeding had bestowed upon it.

"Well, isn't that pervy, not to mention incredibly

The Nookienomicon

rude?" remarked Melvin, still gasping for air.

"This explains why they weren't just running bipedally," breathed Fanny. "Is it normal for men to have five of those?"

"Not human men," replied her husband. "His trousers must fit him like a glove...darling, are you disappointed?"

"No, I'm still trying to figure out how to make them back off!" snapped the young woman. "Honey, give me your sketchbook."

"What are you..."

"Now!"

Still in shock by the sum total of the morning's misadventures, Melvin handed his precious book to his spouse. She flipped it open to a blank page, then ripped out a sheet.

"Hey!" protested the aspiring artist. "I told you I wasn't going to tear one off in public..."

Ignoring her husband's annoyance, Fanny folded the paper into a tiny aeroplane, took aim, and launched it. The makeshift missile hit the fishy flasher squarely in one of its five nether appendages, causing the creature to let out a loud squall. It curled up into the fetal position, buying time for the couple to grab more pages.

The air was soon filled with tiny soaring paper aircraft, reducing the monsters to a confused mob. The Futterbucks pushed their way past the throng, pelted down a pathway called Fish Street, and didn't stop until they saw signs of commerce.

***

The Nookienomicon

"Thank goodness we seem to have lost them," panted Melvin. "What on earth did they want with us, anyway?"

"Didn't you hear them speak? They were paying attention to our conversation. One of them said 'mgshugnah,' which is their word for 'hole'," said Fanny. "Maybe there's something they want with Lady Chatterly, and I suppose they figured we were the liaison."

"My dear, there's no way you could know such a silly thing," replied her husband in a stern tone. "Come on, let's have a look at some of those shops up ahead."

***

"This section of town seems so dreary," moaned Fanny. "Are you certain we'll find any place remotely aseptic where we might consummate our marriage?"

Melvin pointed to a sign. "Look at this place. The Bearded Clam seems like a perfectly fine inn."

"It's doesn't look very sanitary, but none of these accommodations seem to be doing much business. I just don't understand how Lady Chatterly gets any tenants at all. And that's assuming that she really doesn't have multiple mouths, or a dreadful blowhole on the top of her head…"

"Excuse me, good people," croaked a voice that seemed to come from a nearby light post. Mr. and Mrs. Futterbuck jumped at the unexpected intrusion as a tall, rangy man emerged from fog. He seemed impervious to the cold New England weather, with

The Nookienomicon

his shirt unbuttoned at the top and bare head sporting a mop of sable curls.

"I couldn't help but overhear your description of a certain woman," the newcomer ventured, stroking his moustache. "I have heard rumours about this proprietress, and I happen to be a private investigator…"

"You investigate what?" breathed Fanny.

The man sighed. "I'm a detective," he clarified, "specifically into the paranormal and arcane. The name is Holmes."

"Holmes?" breathed Fanny. "Are you of the famous family? Would your name be Sherlock? Or perhaps Mycroft?"

Holmes shuffled his feet. "Actually, it's John."

Fanny gave him a quick appraising glance. "Well then, John Holmes. You certainly seem well-endowed…with your instincts."

"I am trained in the arts," the newcomer said proudly. "Why don't we find a warmer spot, like a pub, where we can speak of this at length?"

"Not a pub, it'll be too noisy," Melvin thought aloud. "How about that café over there?" He pointed to a sign that sported a coffee cup and a smiling figure that was half-human, half-fish, wearing a starred headpiece.

"Nobody's going to buy coffee at a place where the logo is a partially ichthyoid creature," was Fanny's critical observation. "I hope they don't try to franchise it." But the trio found it to be the least forbidding business in town thus far, so they wandered in, ordered hot drinks, and made their way to a booth in the farthest corner.

The Nookienomicon

The Futterbucks regaled John Holmes with their lacklustre honeymoon, the blabbering owner of Gilman House, and ended with their self-defenestration and subsequent chase by the strange fish-frog men.

Holmes' eyes lit up. "Mmmm, I like the Deep Ones," he purred.

Melvin rolled his eyes. "Is this really a necessary thing to disclose to a pair of newlyweds having such a frustrating time of their own?"

Holmes held up a hand in deference. "No, I mean, that's what the race of these fishy-looking citizens are called. Highly intelligent, which you'll come to realise if you get around to understanding what they're saying. Serving Father Dagon, Mother Hydra, and Cthulhu, you won't find fiercer opponents to the Old Gods. They mostly dwell in the undersea metropolis of Y'ha-nthlei, but come ashore to breed with humans. It's not a bad idea, mixing races like that. After all, inbreeding leads to some pretty hideous features over time!"

Fanny opened her lips as if to speak, appeared to change her mind, and instead stammered, "And you're fond of these Deep Ones because…?"

"They're the only beings that can handle my immense talents. Do you want to know why they all have bulging eyes?"

"Not really," said Fanny with a pucker.

"There's a good bit of lore about them in this grimoire I always carry with me." He dug into his coat and showed them a leather-bound tome. "The Nookienomicon!" he announced with no small amount of pride.

The Nookienomicon

Melvin peered at one of the pages he revealed. "It's an awfully strange-looking written language," he observed. "Lots of apostrophes...perhaps indicating glottal stops?"

"It looks more like a Comma Sutra," supplied Fanny, but the men were already on another tangent.

"So might I ask about Lady Chatterly?" pressed Holmes. "What did she speak of?"

Melvin wrung his gloved hands. "We don't actually know. She nattered on for so long, it's like it made us both fall into a trance."

Holmes's eyes sparkled. "It appears that her talent for nattering makes mortals daydream themselves into an infernal dimension. Such is the way of people touched by the Old Ones."

"Touched by the Old Ones?" Fanny looked delightedly aghast. "In what way? Can you show me on a doll?"

"Let me rephrase that. There are real-life monsters out there, including Elder Gods that would cause a mortal to lose his mind. Some people have dalliances with them, resulting in madness, or at least odd speech patterns. If I can plant a recording device somewhere, I might be able to analyse whatever it is about her speech that is preventing you from burying the bishop..."

Fanny's swollen lips fell into a pout. "But then we won't have the entire chess set!"

Holmes' temples flared. "Never mind. Now if I might accompany you back to the hotel, we can get started."

Fanny beamed. "Okay, but I get to be in the

The Nookienomicon

middle!"

The detective looked stern. "My dear, this is a matter of solving a mystery!"

"Precisely. People always leave the women out of such things, and I want to be in on all the action."

"Very well," Holmes acquiesced. "You might be able to get some answers. Or at least a way to shut her up. For a small fee, or perhaps an exchange of favours, I could be of great service to you." Fanny giggled, then appeared crestfallen when Holmes' hungry gaze fell upon her husband.

"No bartering," growled Melvin. "We're going to pay you properly, and as a token of good faith, we'll take care of the bill at this café."

Holmes sighed. "Can I at least put the tip in?"

***

Lady Chatterly was in her usual spot in the foyer when they entered. She did not even seem to remember losing the newlyweds that very morning, nor did she bother to introduce herself to the newcomer, so intent was she on sustaining her babble.

"Can you believe that someone claimed to have spotted a rat the other day?" she gabbled. "Why, we haven't had any sort of small mammals in Innsmouth since my great-grandfather quit his job as a clock winder. Not that anyone pays attention to timepieces. Around here they just show up at the rituals, sometimes a minute early, maybe even off by ten minutes…"

Holmes's entire body suddenly went rigid.

The Nookienomicon

"Goodness me, his entire length is stiff!" gasped Fanny.

Holmes began to thrash and convulse, while Melvin barked, "He's having fits! Lady Chatterly, do you have any smelling salts?"

The proprietress sprang to her feet. "I've just the thing! I'll be back in two shakes, if you'll excuse the expression!"

As soon as she swept down the hall, Holmes bolted for Lady Chatterly's cathedra.

"I noticed the way she was sitting in her chair, and I've found a secret spot between the legs!" he hissed.

"Nonsense, I've always heard men can't find that," sighed Fanny.

"No, the legs of her chair. There's a hollow place where I can install this wax cylinder recording device."

Melvin's brow furrowed. "Do women typically wax their seats?"

"You tell me," grumbled Holmes, fiddling with some wires to keep the device hidden. "You're the one who's honeymooning."

"No, I mean their stools!"

"I don't know anything about their stools. You'll have to ask a chambermaid. Okay, the device is recording. Get it back to me first thing in the morning, and I'll see if I can detect anything unusual in her speech."

He tipped the brim of his hat and beat a hasty retreat as the hotel owner returned, saying, "...could have been a movie star, but he couldn't stay away from fish. Now down at the wharf, there's another

The Nookienomicon

fellow who just sits there drinking whiskey, and I remember his mother from the old church. She's one of the Marsh family, and I always said that if you're a Marsh, you're guaranteed acceptance to Miskatonic University. It's pure nepotism, if you ask me…"

And Lady Chatterly resumed her usual chinwag. Mr. and Mrs. Futterbuck, drawn into the same stupor as before, wasted another evening with their flowers of innocence intact. *Let's hope the device between her legs is working,* thought Melvin as they managed to drag themselves up the stairs and into their room before unconsciousness overtook them both.

***

The cheerless, watery morning light did nothing to mar Lady Chatterly's mood as the Futterbucks descended the stairs the following day. She was in her usual cathedra chair in the foyer, a gold crown peeking out from beneath her starred pillbox hat. The couple braced themselves for the plan they were determined to carry out.

"Do you like my new tiara?" squealed the proprietress. "Can you believe some of the townsfolk in Arkham find them to be unfashionable? Why, not even some of the debutantes down south could even…"

Husband and wife gritted their teeth and fought to stay alert. They had to retrieve the device, and getting a word in edgewise long enough to distract her wouldn't be easy.

The Nookienomicon

"...they come to the shore and spawn with the humans. The offspring develop features of these fish-frog men, and they end up living forever. I've had many men in my time, but if you close your eyes and ignore the smell, one of those Deep Ones is as good a roll in the seaweed as any..."

"Wait, what?" Melvin blurted out.

"Close your eyes and ignore the smell!" yapped Lady Chatterly, paying attention to her guests' cues for once. "Isn't that what they tell all men before they get married?"

"Oh, for the love of Dagon..." grumbled Fanny, rising to her feet and trotting to an umbrella stand in the corner of the foyer. Grabbing a bone-handled walking cane, she flounced back and swung it against the back of Lady Chatterly's skull. The buxom woman slumped in her chair, her speech slurring into silence like a gramophone unplugged — "A rolllll... in the seeee... weeeeed..." — letting her hat fall off and exposing her bare head.

Sure enough, there was a gaping hole where the top of her skull should have been.

"We were right," frowned Fanny. "She's got an extra mouth, with rows and rows of teeth. And the breath is so terrible, that hole really could use a..."

Doosh! A loud crash made the newlyweds jump to their feet.

Holmes came rushing in the door. "Sorry about the bad parking job, but it was a tight squeeze and I didn't have much time. Have you got the cylinder?"

"We didn't have a chance to remove it," groaned Melvin. "You're the one who knows how this device works anyway."

The Nookienomicon

In a trice Holmes was at the chair, on his knees and fiddling between the legs. He removed the apparatus and the cylinder, hissing, "Quickly, let's go to the room."

"First, we stop up that extra mouth," suggested Melvin. He grabbed the closest object he could find, the globe of a Victorian piano lamp, and rammed it tightly into the horrifying maw that Lady Chatterly's hat normally concealed.

The trio charged up the stairs, their hostess still out cold.

As they locked the door, Holmes produced the Nookienomicon and an incense ball from his bag. He lit the herbs inside and cast a salt circle around them. "This will purify the room of any foul taint brought in by the Old Ones." Opening the Nookienomicon, he chanted some incantations before his shoulders dropped in relief at this safety precaution. "We should be protected for a short time," he huffed, "but let's not tarry." The private investigator reached into his bag again, produced a splendid phonograph bell, and attached it to the recording device.

The trio gathered around the phonograph and held their breaths. They strained to catch any sounds as Holmes turned the crank.

"How strange," murmured the detective. "This recording is almost nothing but silence! Most curious that it didn't record the incessant chatter, but just as well we don't have to hear it a second time. But every now and then, tiny syllables became audible. Can somebody write them down?"

Fanny snatched her husband's sketchbook and

The Nookienomicon

began scribbling furiously. "When strung together, it's a message that says, 'Mgahnnn ya yogfm'l l'ymg' gotha'!" she crowed in triumph.

The two men stared at her blankly.

Fanny pursed her lips together. "That sounds like the R'lyehian language. It means, 'Open my star to your desires'."

A loud banging downstairs made them all jump. The trio looked out the window to see a dozen stout Deep Ones gathered on the street, dressed in the same clerical robes. There was another bang, then they heard the door creak open to the monologue of, "...oh yes, I was just talking about what a delight it is to have you visitors. Why, even my own auntie used to regale me with tales of you people...I believe this was when I was about fifteen years of age, maybe sixteen..."

Holmes bolted for the door, swinging it open with a maddened hubris. "The time has come for glory!" he bellowed, charging down the stairs. The Futterbucks, terrified as they were, made their way after the detective, unsure which was worse: the infernal-looking creatures from some ghastly dimension or the prospect of having to hear Lady Chatterly once more.

A split second later, a fine sheet of mist came in through the doorway, soaking the lobby. "Look at what you've done!" Melvin chided the intruders. "You're leaving a stain on the carpet, and now my Fanny is wet!"

Holmes began to quiver. Producing a gold circlet from his pocket, he held it to the light like a protective talisman.

The Nookienomicon

"How is a bracelet going to save us?" Melvin bellowed.

"It's not a bracelet. It helps me maintain control when I interact with these lovely…uh, I mean, vile abominations."

"I actually think their fish heads are quite handsome," cooed Fanny.

"Eat them up, yum," agreed Lady Chatterly, oblivious to the glass globe still lodged in the top of her head. "Actually, I've been known to make a decent chowder, although I wouldn't dare tell our new friends what the ingredients are. Mister Futterbuck, does your Fanny produce a good sauce?"

"Why won't she shut the sodding hell up?" snarled Melvin. "We've already plugged her hole."

But Lady Chatterly didn't stop with her mere babbling. Holmes, panicking, lobbed his incense ball at her feet. As the smoke fell around her, she began to transform, her body bursting through the seams of her dress. Creamy skin filmed over into murky protoplasm. And it just so happened that she had yet another mouth, and another, and two dozen more…

"Shoggoth!" screamed Holmes. "She's been disguised as a human this entire time!"

The amorphous creature turned its myriad eyes on the three humans. "I don't know what you're on about," Lady Chatterly's unmistakable voice resonated from one of the creature's two dozen mouths. "Maybe I could take the shape of something cuter?" The shoggoth squeezed its gelatinous flesh into something vaguely bivalve-

The Nookienomicon

shaped. "How do you do?" the enormous shell-shaped being piped up. "I'm not going to clam up anytime soon! Ah, that's a good one, isn't it?"

The newlywed Mrs. Futterbuck was sceptical. "Actually, that looks more like a..."

"Fanny!" Melvin came to his senses. "How do you know R'lyehian? And why aren't the fish-frog men attacking you?"

"Not to mention that she's not screaming in terror," chimed in Holmes. "She actually seems rather aroused. Is this what it takes to make Fanny fresh?"

"You're not so pristine yourself!" snapped Fanny. "You cleaned your foul taint in our room just now. Go on, then, now that you've summoned one of the arcane, what are you going to do?"

John Holmes rolled his eyes, unzipped his trousers, and a cephalopod arm the length of a baseball bat fell out.

"I suppose it's time to find out which one of those holes is doing all the talking." The couple stood slack-jawed as Holmes defensively snapped, "Well, I'm not going to put my hand in those mouths!"

What happened next was something husband and wife seemed to remember differently. Fanny watched transfixed as Holmes explored every orifice of the giant amoeba, engaging in some sort of activity she had only seen dogs do in the parks. But Melvin could have sworn he saw visions of some giant creature rising from the sea. The monster appeared to be part man, part octopus, and part dragon. Its octopine eyes went wide, then it

The Nookienomicon

clapped its webbed claws over what were presumably ears and gave a mighty roar.

The words sounded clearly in his mind. *In His House at R'lyeh Dead Cthulhu waits dreaming. Yet the prattle has awoken him, and he's quite miffed about it...*

The three mortals heard a distant rumbling and something that sounded like, "Mgah! H'uaaah mgah!"

"That means 'Stop! Make it stop!'" Fanny hissed. "Honey, what are you doing? We're supposed to be saving the world, and you're doodling in your sketchbook?"

"It's not doodling!" snapped her husband. "I have to preserve these visions. They will inspire the greatest paintings someday!"

The shoggoth's yakking never ceased: "...he's dead but he's also dreaming, and that doesn't seem possible to a human, but when I was a little girl, I once saw a..."

Melvin bawled, "Holmes! This is your job! If you don't find a way to get this tiresome shoggoth to shut up, one of the Great Old Ones is going to take matters into His claws!"

"I'm trying, all right?" shot back a muffled retort from somewhere in the gelatinous abomination. "This isn't exactly playing a round of golf! Who knows how many holes are in this thing?"

Fanny shouted, "Ymg' mguln ph'nglui ymg' n'ghft, f'narr f'narr f'narr!" She turned to her husband and beamed proudly. "That means, 'banish yourself into your dark pit!'"

At once, the wretched creatures of the deep

The Nookienomicon

turned to face the haranguing shoggoth. One by one they climbed atop every surface of her, searching for any mouth that might be the source of the infernal speech. They rolled their bulging eyes in exasperation as they all began to mimic Holmes. This was one game of stationary leapfrog the couple hoped they'd never have to witness again.

"It's like a giant spotted dick," observed Melvin.

"I suppose I'd contract diseases myself if I had to engage in congress with that tiresome blob," agreed his wife.

"Well, whatever you chanted seems to be working. It's like she's trying to devour herself. And the fish-frog men appear to be either eager or suicidal."

"No, they're just as desperate to shut her up as any living thing."

"Now that's what I call teamwork!" crowed Melvin.

Before long the shoggoth was covered in ichthyoid men. With no recognizable facial features, it nonetheless seemed to be enjoying itself, moaning, "Iä! Iä! Iä!"

"Look out, Holmes!" cried Fanny. "You'll be crushed!"

The sole human voice gasped, "Well, I'm trying to get off!"

"Then close your eyes and think about your first naughty dream!" suggested Melvin.

With a sickening crunch, the mass of bodies widened the doorway of the hotel, leaving behind a gaping hole in the splintered frame and crumbled bricks. The giant blob that was Lady Chatterly oozed out of the front door of Gilman House, still covered with writhing Deep Ones and one nearly human detective.

The Futterbucks ran back upstairs to watch the cluster ooze away from them. The protean form made its way down to the harbour with only one final guttural croon: "A rolllll… in the seeeeeea… weeeeeed…" There was a hollow, wet sound like a giant bottle being corked, and then the voices ceased at long last. The terrifying orgy plopped itself into the ocean, causing a noxious wave of brackish water to slam onto the shoreline, then all was still. Only the echo of a delighted cackle came from somewhere in the direction of Devil Reef.

For a long time, neither husband nor wife spoke. They savoured the silence that had fallen across the bleak little town on Innsmouth, more welcome than any unlikely beam of sunlight.

"You never did tell me where you learned to speak that ancient language," accused Melvin lightly.

Fanny shrugged. "What else is there to talk about in Girl Scouts? Everyone thinks we talk about boys while we sit around making pinecone bird feeders."

***

The bus destined for Niagara Falls rolled up just in time for the newlyweds to grab their luggage and head for the unknown.

"Well, we might still need to find another place to consummate our marriage, but at least we managed to save this land from being consumed by

The Nookienomicon

the Elder Gods," chuckled Melvin. "I'm still slightly concerned about your affinity for the language, but we have a few years yet before we discover whether or not you develop the Innsmouth look."

"If I do, might I remind you that there could be a few advantages?" purred Fanny. "At least if we turn out the lights."

"Mmm, I suppose so, darling. Just don't summon anything, okay?"

Fanny frowned. "What would it take to make the Old Ones come?" she wondered aloud.

"Twenty outboard motors and the hull of an old rocket?" guessed her husband.

They both burst out laughing. "Very well!" Fanny gushed. "Carry on, Lady Chatterly!"

The Nookienomicon

V

Two's Company, Three's A Crowd, A Cult's A Blooming Gangb...
By David Green

Tenerife, July 1971.

"Cor, look at them baps!" Jeff cried, striding into the breakfast room at the Dagon Hotel, eyes dancing with delight.

"Oh, you dirty old bugger," a woman in a Polka Dot bikini huffed, covering her breasts with her hands, and not having much success doing so.

"What you on about?" Jeff pushed past her, grabbing a plate from the end of the table. "Continental breakfast, bloody love 'em!"

He grabbed a handful of baps from the spread, loading them onto his plate, mind already on the heaps of sausage and bacon. Funny thing, continental breakfasts. Stick a load of fruit, yogurts, pastries, and salads on them, and the sodding English will always wander on by and stuff their faces with the greasiest food available.

"Oh," the woman muttered, lowering her hands, cheeks more than a little rosy. "I thought you meant... name's Loretta."

"Charmed," Jeff replied, looking over his shoulder and giving her the once over. "Any coffee going?"

"Table over there," she replied, standing on her tiptoes and pointing across the breakfast room. "'Ere, you from Manchester?"

The Nookienomicon

"Aye," Jeff answered, distracted, as he looked for the brown HP sauce. "Reckon you're from Stockport."

"Cheeky beggar! Manchester too, love. You here alone?"

Jeff smiled his most winning smile. The one he reckoned the ladies loved. "Not anymore."

***

The sun beat down from above. Jeff, tanned already but oiled up just the same, sat on his sun lounger, reading *The Sun* from back home in good old Blighty. Well, reading is a subjective term. He'd been admiring the talent on show on Page Three for a good ten minutes.

"Oh, give over," Loretta huffed, slapping his forearm. "You're going to burn holes in that page."

"Yeah," Jeff laughed, turning the paper to her, "two of them. Big ones!"

Loretta giggled. "Ooh, that sun *is* hot. I'm burning up. Mind putting some lotion on my back?"

She didn't wait for a yes. Now, Jeff fancied himself a ladies' man, and never had to look far for a bit of new totty, and never stayed about too long after, but he had to admit, Loretta had grown on him.

Literally.

He ogled her as she spun around on her front, feet in the air, and reached to undo her bikini top. She let it fall to the side and looked over her shoulder, a wicked smile on her lips. "Well, you up for it?"

The Nookienomicon

"Rather," Jeff growled, standing to attention in more places than one.

Loretta's throaty chuckle didn't help matters.

He scooped up the lotion and straddled her, squirting the cream onto her back and rubbing it in, savouring the feel of her skin.

"Here, stop digging into my back, will you?" Loretta laughed, kicking his behind with her feet.

Jeff took his mind off pressing matters. He nodded at a waiter from Hotel Dagon, making the universal, *'come here and give me a fresh drink'* sign.

A black-robed figure appeared, face hidden in the shadows. It stood before Jeff and Loretta in silence, the sounds of the waves sloshing against the beach and holidaymakers frolicking in the pool seeming distant and foreign.

"Pina Colada, mate," Jeff muttered when the waiter still didn't talk. "At least, I think it's mate. Madam?"

"And for the lady?" came a deep, wet hiss. Male, then.

"G and T, love," Loretta said without looking up.

The waiter's hood inclined. A nod, Jeff reckoned, before he moved away without another word.

"'Ere," Jeff grumbled, tapping Loretta on her lotion-slick shoulder. "You noticed anything weird about this place?"

"What, other than the name?" she answered, head still on its side. "Hotel Dagon, gives me the willies. It's cheap. It's in the sun. Company isn't so bad."

The Nookienomicon

"The willies, eh?" Jeff smiled, but, for once, his heart wasn't in it. "You don't think those waiters are sweltering in those black robes? They're all in 'em."

"Foreigners, aren't they? What's hot for us is like winter for them. Relax, love. Let's have another few drinks then get in, out of the sun for a bit." She peered over her shoulder, lowered her sunglasses, and winked.

Jeff's craggy face broke out into a grin. "Your room or mine?"

"There's time for both, love," she giggled.

Jeff's laughter faded as he turned his attention to the waiters again. Black robes sliding across the pool area, silent, watching, shadowed.

"Your drinks, sir," came a hiss by his side.

"Cripes, man," Jeff yelled, hand on his chest, "where'd you come from? Almost gave me a sodding heart attack!"

The waiter set down a tray with the refreshments and moved away, bowing. But Jeff had no eyes for his Pina Colada. He'd seen the man's hand as it slipped from his robe. Pasty white, and slimy like a fish, with nails as black as midnight.

"Willies is right," he muttered, shivering despite the heat.

Jeff settled back on his lounger, drink in one hand, newspaper in the other, but he didn't read it. Not even page three. No, he watched the workers of Hotel Dagon, and tried to figure out what their game was.

***

The Nookienomicon

"What's on the menu tonight, then? Fish again, is it?"

Since the morning on the beach, Jeff had kept his eye on the workers at the Hotel Dagon. Loretta seemed oblivious to their odd goings on, but not him. One thing he'd noticed, something that had passed him by on his first few days on holiday, was that other than the continental breakfast, all the food the hotel served contained fish.

"Oh, Jeff, give over, would you? These lads are probably paid a pittance. They don't need to hear your moaning all day," Loretta sighed, turning her smile to the hooded figure. "Just bring us anything you think's nice, dear. And a couple more cocktails, there's a love."

The figure bowed without a word, gliding backwards and away into the kitchens. Jeff's eyes narrowed as the doors remained open a touch; he saw two of the workers, covered heads close together, whispering. He couldn't tell for certain, but he reckoned they were talking about him. Jeff shook his head. Maybe the sun cooked his brains. Like Loretta said, foreigners weren't half a queer bunch.

"What do you do for a living, anyway?" he asked, lighting a cigarette and winking. "Apart from me, that is."

"Cheeky," Loretta laughed. "I'm a lady of leisure!"

"Rich daddy?"

"There's been a few, but a lady never tells her number."

The Nookienomicon

"No," Jeff laughed, shaking his head, "I meant your father."

"Oh, silly me." Loretta winked. "He lives in Spain. I'm over here visiting and fancied a quick holiday."

"Lives in Spain, eh?" Jeff muttered. "That's the life. What does he do?"

"He breeds bulls. He ships 50,000 to South America every year."

Jeff raised his eyebrows. "That's a lot of bulls."

Loretta beamed back at him. "He's the biggest bullshipper around."

"I'd say," Jeff replied, stifling a laugh. "Look out, they're bringing our drinks. Keep your peepers out, see if there's anything unusual."

Jeff ignored her sigh. He'd noticed something strange already. Normally, the black-robed waiters slid across the floor, but this one *swayed*. Smaller than the others, too. The figure carried their drinks on a tray with one hand, and came to a stop before them, and removed the hood.

Jeff's temperature went up a degree.

A woman, a beautiful one, smiled demurely at him. Olive skinned, her luscious black locks fell down her back now she'd removed her hood. Eyes so dark they appeared purple sparkled at him, and lips as red as cherries parted, inviting him to kiss them.

"Close your jaw, Jeff," Loretta grumbled, "it's rude to gawp."

His teeth clicked as he snapped his mouth shut. The woman leaned forward to rest the drinks on a table. A slither of bare leg appeared through her

The Nookienomicon

parted robe, her foot arched and toes painted red.

"Would you like anything else?" she asked, staring at him over the cocktails.

"Rather," Jeff stuttered, fiery blood rushing to his extremities.

"You've done enough, love," Loretta grimaced, kicking Jeff under the table. "Why don't you go back to wherever you came from?"

The woman ignored her, looking only at Jeff, who stared back, moon-eyed and slack faced. "My name is Chastity. I shall be yours for the evening. Call me if you require anything. Anything at all."

With a smile, she turned, hips swaying as she headed for the kitchen. She glanced over her shoulder, flashing Jeff a smile that was anything but chaste.

"Blimey!" Jeff exclaimed, gulping down his Pina Colada. "When did they upgrade the staff?"

"Hmm, you call that an upgrade?" Loretta grumbled, twisting the straw in her drink, eyes throwing daggers at Jeff. "I reckon you're right, there's something fishy going on here."

He ignored her. Chastity smiled once more before she disappeared into the kitchens, and Jeff downed his drink, signalling another black-robed figure for another. He'd drink the place dry if the woman kept bringing him drinks, and eat as much fish as they fed him. So long as *she* brought it.

***

Loretta headed back to her room alone after Jeff decided on a nightcap at the bar, his new favourite

The Nookienomicon

waitress fawning all over him.

"Nightcap?" she'd muttered, scowling at the pair. "Don't think either of you are thinking about caps tonight!"

She'd ignored Jeff's suspicions about Hotel Dagon throughout the holiday, putting it down to a typical British man's distrust of foreigners, which she always laughed at. The lads would grumble about every other country's odd ways, or the how 'Johnny Foreigner' would come over and steal their jobs—which most of the lazy English bastards didn't want to do anyway—or carry on with their women, but it didn't stop them all from jetting off to Spain, Malta, or Greece for the jollies, did it?

And then have the cheek to complain about their foreign ways and too-flavoursome food while they were there!

"Well, I'm not going chasing after Jeff," Loretta grumbled to herself, staring down a long, dark corridor, its crimson carpets and matching paper making her shudder. "But I think he *was* right about this place. It really is odd. The booking agent said the place was almost sold out, but there's never anyone around except for me, Jeff, the workers, and a few others."

Right on cue, a blood-curdling cry echoed from behind a closed door ahead of Loretta. She flattened herself against the wall, suddenly aware she only wore a pink bikini. Funny, the things that pop into people's heads in times of danger.

The door tore open, and a harried looking man came barrelling out, neat greying hair wild, and blue eyes just as crazy. He slammed the door behind him

The Nookienomicon

and turned, panting. In his hands, he clutched a leather-bound book, and he wore a robe at least one size too small for him, and nothing else. His stare fell on Loretta.

"I need you!" he yelled, pointing a trembling finger.

Loretta covered her breasts with her hands and tried to cross her legs. "Oh, give over! I'm spoken for!"

"Not like that, you old bat!" he sneered, peering down his long nose, nostrils flaring. "You're sex mad! Everyone here is sex mad!"

"Chance would be a fine thing," Loretta grumbled, thinking of Jeff and Chastity in the bar below. "What do you want, anyway?"

"Hide me, woman," the man cried, almost on his knees, begging, despite the superior cast to his features. Loretta reckoned that was just the way his face looked. He could be caught naked in a snowstorm, gentleman's bits frozen and shrivelled, and he'd still look like the King of England. "Please! And take this book. It's driving the women who work here crazy! Oh, the things she wanted to do!"

He shoved the tome into her hands. Loretta's fingers itched from touching it. It looked like leather, but it felt... odd. Wrinklier. Like an old man. She shivered and glanced at the title.

"The Nookinomicon?" she asked, raising an eyebrow. "Sounds interesting."

"Oh, not you, too. Come on, let's go to your room, I'll fill you in."

"Now who's sex mad?" Loretta tittered.

The Nookienomicon

The man's nostrils flared again, a look of outraged shock crossing his face. "Madam, I have no interest in *that* with *you* whatsoever. But we're all in danger if we stay in the Hotel Dagon any longer! We must escape!"

Loretta eyed the corridor again. Her doubts about the place kept piling up. The man seemed frazzled but didn't strike her as a liar.

"Alright," she sighed, clutching the book against her breasts. "Come on. But no funny business!"

"Oh, thank you," the man breathed, hopping from foot to foot like he needed the toilet. "No funny business, scout's honour. My name's Kenny, by the way."

The door rattled, causing the pair to jump.

"This way," Loretta whispered, heading off with Kenny in tow, "we can do introductions later."

***

"Do you enjoy reading, Jeff?" Chastity crooned, staring at him with those beautiful, dark eyes. He could lose himself in them if he weren't careful.

But would he mind getting lost? Not half.

"Prefer looking at the pictures," Jeff laughed, sipping at another Pina Colada. He frowned. They'd kept coming all night without him ordering. "Maybe Loretta…"

His frown deepened. Loretta. Where'd she get to? He half-turned, but Chastity's soft fingers on his cheek stopped him.

"You like the pictures, you wicked man," she cooed, a twinkle in those dark pools. "I have just the

The Nookienomicon

thing for you."

She withdrew her fingers, leaving a damp patch on Jeff's cheek. He paid it no mind, as she reached under her robe and produced a thick, heavy looking book, bound in leather.

"You keeping anything else up there you'd like to share?" he asked, laughing at his own joke.

Chastity smiled. "Perhaps you'll be so lucky. This is the Nookinomicon. With this, it won't only be the drinks coming all night."

Jeff downed his drink.

***

"So, what exactly are you saying? That this hotel is a front for some kind of… sex cult? Maybe they should charge more!"

Loretta lay on the bed, stomach flat against the mattress, feet kicking behind her, and flicked through the Nookinomicon. Kenny's eyes darted to every corner of her room. Everywhere, that is, except for her, and her underwear and bikinis strewn here and there.

Loretta wasn't the tidiest of people, so this proved a hard feat to achieve.

"Oh, you wicked woman," he hissed, nostrils flaring again. "You're one of them, aren't you? Sent to test me. Lord above, save me!"

Loretta eyed his crotch pointedly. "Something below's stirring, you old dog. I think you rather enjoy all of this."

"I do not!" Kenny cried, bending over to hide the growing rise in his underwear. "Don't you have some clothes for me to wear?"

"You can have one of my bikinis if you like?" Loretta laughed and chuckled harder when the frazzled man's cheeks turned a deeper shade of red. "I think one of the yellow ones would suit you!"

"Now you look here—"

Loretta nodded at the spare bed and winked. "Take the bedsheet."

With a huff, Kenny stalked across to it, whipping the sheet off the mattress and wrapping it around himself. Covered, his colour returned to normal, and he stood straight-backed, head tilted slightly, his face haughty, looking every inch a pauper Roman Emperor.

"What I am saying, dear," he began, nostrils flaring again. Loretta stared at them and wondered if anyone had ever stuck a grape up there. "Is that we're all in danger. If it were just a bit of hanky panky between the staff and holidaymakers, it would be bad enough. But it's *everyone. All* of the *time.* Do you see anyone roaming the halls? Anyone at the pool, or at the bar for more than a day? No. They're seduced. It's not… it's not…"

"Right?" Loretta suggested.

"British," Kenny finished with a nod.

"Oh, lord." Loretta rolled her eyes. "Not you, too. Only because something isn't *British* doesn't mean it's wrong or evil. This is just a funny little sex book. Some of the positions seem quite interesting, really, if you'd like to…"

The words died in her mouth as her eyes fell to the page she'd flicked to. It showed a woman straddling a man in the throes of passion. Strange

The Nookienomicon

symbols surrounded them, and people in black robes, watching their lovemaking, knives in their hands.

"Kinky," she breathed, trying to make her voice light, but ice settled in her stomach.

"Turn the page," Kenny commanded, looking like a back-market Caligula, "then you'll see I'm right."

Her hands flew to her mouth. The man still lay on the floor, but agony instead of pleasure stood out on his face. He'd been cut open, his entrails and organs pulled from his body and stretched so they touched the strange symbols. Where the black-robed people had stood in the last drawing lay shadow, and from it, creeping and writhing—the picture seemed to move as she examined it. Impossible, she knew—long tentacles reached towards him.

Loretta shut the book with a snap. "We need to find Jeff."

"Jeff?" Kenny barked, his makeshift robe slipping. "Jeff? We need to *leave*!"

***

"Excuse me, love, got an itch on my nose. Don't suppose you could…"

As far as compromising positions went, Jeff couldn't think of many he'd preferred to be in.

Stretched out on a creaking, four-poster bed, the sheets and covers the same dark red and black that the owner of the Hotel Dagon appeared to enjoy, restraints tied to Jeff's wrists and ankles holding him in place. Naked, save for a pair of red Speedos.

The Nookienomicon

He wrinkled his nose. "I mean, it really is quite distracting."

Chastity stood at the bed's end, long pale leg bare, the rest of her hidden in the black robe. Except her face. She smiled at him, a smile that suggested she knew a secret no-one else did.

Cor, it really got Jeff going.

He'd always gone for simpering types, women who needed a man in their life. Any man would do, so long as he came home at night, and ate the food they'd make. This one, Chastity, she wasn't like the others at all. Confident. Intelligent. Mysterious! And beautiful. Blimey, was she? Loretta seemed a bit different, too. Not like Chastity, but a cut above the rest. She'd made him laugh, and the things she could do in bed…

"Do you know where my friend's got to? The small, blonde, busty one. Enjoyed wearing a bikini and not much else."

Chastity's dark eyes shone. "You dare speak of other women in my presence, you naughty boy?"

"Well—"

"Enough, let us begin."

Jeff laughed. "What? No foreplay? Where've you been all my life?"

"Here, in service of my lord."

"You know," Jeff muttered, twitching his nose again. That damned itch! "You didn't really strike me as the religious type. Though it explains the robes."

"We usually don't go so far into the Nookinomicon so early, with someone so new. But I believe you're ready for it," Chastity whispered.

The Nookienomicon

Jeff wondered if she could hear him speak at all. "And my lord hungers. Soon, he'll wake, and you'll have played your part."

"Planning on getting noisy, are we?" Jeff laughed, Speedos getting tight.

They soon deflated.

From the shadows surrounding the bed, robed figures stepped forward, chanting in God knows what language.

"Er—" Jeff began, his tent pole in need of major renovation.

Chastity dropped her robe. Jeff screamed. A blood-curdling, horrified, terrified scream. Instead of looking like the lovely lasses on page three, the ones Jeff knew so well, she stood there, half-woman, half-octopus. Tentacles extended from beneath her breasts, scales covered her skin from the neck below, and she slithered onto the bed.

A slimy, wet tentacle caressed Jeff's leg, and he screamed again, working his leg, trying to get it away or loose in vain.

"I demand to see your manager," he cried, jerking his arms, rattling the bed's headboard. "This wasn't in the brochures!"

The chanting grew louder, as did Jeff's cries for help.

***

Loretta and Kenny raced through the long, crimson corridors, squeals of delight coming from behind the closed doors.

And the occasional howls of pain and terror.

The Nookienomicon

"Sounds like they're all at it tonight," Loretta shouted, her heeled shoes clipping. Kenny had begged her to dress in more than her customary bikini and flip-flops, so she'd put her see-through nightie on, too.

Anything to keep his nostrils from flaring. Not like it had worked. Kenny had gone an even paler shade of white, his eyes wider than the holes in his nose. Despite their circumstances, Loretta couldn't help but giggle.

Kenny huffed as he struggled to keep up with her pace. "I don't see why we need to rescue Jeff. He got into this mess himself, chasing after women all the time. Especially when he was with you."

Loretta paused, her cheeks a little red. A compliment? From Kenny? "Thank you, sweetheart."

"Well, it's just... I mean..."

Loretta reached her arms up and grabbed Kenny's head, pulling it down and planting a kiss on his lip. He protested at first, squawking like an indignant seagull, but then he relaxed and let his hands wander across her back.

"Steady on," Loretta murmured, giving him a wink. "No time for hanky panky."

"Oh, you devil-woman," Kenny breathed, kissing her again with such ferocity it lifted her feet from the floor.

Loretta nudged him away. "Rescue and escape first. How's your father after."

"I don't see what my father's got to do with anything," Kenny replied, frowning. "He's been dead twenty years."

The Nookienomicon

Loretta laughed. "Kenny, can I ask? Have you ever... been with a woman?"

His frown deepened. "Of course. I've lived with my mother all my life!"

She took his hand, pulling him down the corridor towards Jeff's room.

"This is a holiday I'm not going to forget in a hurry," Loretta laughed, as the doors rattled and the lights in the corridor faded.

Loud chanting took the place of the howls of pleasure and pain, and ice filled her stomach. She almost understood the words, like they danced on the edge of her understanding. They meant nothing good; she knew that much.

"I'll introduce you to my mother, if you like," Kenny said, still visibly confused.

She patted his hand, pulling him up short. "That sounds nice. Right, this is Jeff's room. Follow my lead."

"I'll follow your lead and anything else you'll put in front of me."

Loretta sighed. "Sex mad. Everyone here's sex mad. Must be something in the water."

***

The hooded figures stepped forward, knives in their hands, the blades glinting in the low light of the room.

Chastity straddled Jeff, the tentacles spilling from her midriff writhing. They slithered across his legs, bare chest and arms.

Jeff thanked the Lord above when they avoided

The Nookienomicon

his Speedos, and that area remained thoroughly unexcited.

"Maybe we could start from page one in the Nookinomicon?" he stammered, sweat beading on his forehead. "I think, after all, I'm really not ready for the advanced section."

Chastity gargled in response, an inhuman warble. Her eyes had rolled into the back of her head. White glassy orbs stared at Jeff instead of those dark irises.

The robed figures creeped closer, the chanting rising in volume. He wanted to cover his ears, but try as he might, he couldn't free his wrists.

"This is it then?" Jeff wailed, kicking his legs in vain. "I always wanted to go out on the job, but not like this. Not like this!"

His hotel room door crashed open, light flooding in. The robed figures hissed and skittered away from the light. Chastity's eyes flicked back to normal as she snarled at the intruders.

Loretta stood in the doorway, a skinny and horrified looking man behind her, dressed in nothing but a bedsheet, a copy of the Nookinomicon in hand.

"What a sight for sore eyes you are, love!" Jeff called, before doubt crept into his head. She had the book! "Unless you're... one of them? At least you don't have tentacles."

Loretta strode forward, hefting the book, and slammed it into Chastity's face.

"Get away from him you... whatever in God's name you are!" The tentacled woman slid to the ground, writhing in pain. "Kenny! Come help me with this!"

The Nookienomicon

She worked on Jeff's restraints, pulling his leg free. He howled in pain as blood rushed into his foot, but eyeing the knives the hooded figures still clutched as they kept away from the light, Jeff considered an aching ankle better than the alternative.

"Oh, do I have to?" Kenny complained, pulling at the ties on Jeff's wrists. "I mean, look at him. Could he have found a smaller sized Speedo? It isn't right."

"Give over." Loretta yanked his other leg free just as Kenny finished with his wrists, pulling him from the bed. "He's on holiday."

"Let's get out of here!" Kenny cried, legging it from the room as soon as Jeff's feet touched the floor.

"You know," Jeff said, leaning on Loretta as they slammed the door behind them and followed Kenny, "my mother always warned me I'd meet a woman like you. I must write and thank her."

"Escape first," Loretta laughed, a deep and throaty one, "jokes later."

"About that. Where are we going?"

Loretta shrugged mid run. "No idea, I'm following Kenny."

Behind them, hotel room doors flew open, and black-robed figures spilled out, knives in hands. Chanting.

"Does he have a plan?" Jeff asked, keenly aware he wore nothing but his bright red Speedos that left little to the imagination.

"I hope he bloody has one," Loretta grumbled, eyeing the blades in their hands, "as I really don't fancy one of them inside me."

"Sex mad," Jeff muttered, shaking his head. "Everyone here is bloody sex mad!"

***

"A plan?" Kenny shrieked, racing through the corridors, his borrowed bedsheet flapping. "Why am I the one coming up with a plan?"

"He doesn't have a plan," Jeff shouted over his shoulder.

"I heard!" Loretta yelled, bringing up the rear.

Black-robed villains poured from the doors behind them, knives in their hands, chanting in their strange tongue.

"Bloody foreigners," Jeff shouted. "We just wanted a holiday! I'll tell my travel agent about this!"

They came to the main stairs that led to the Hotel Dagon's foyer. From the corridor facing them, more black-robed figures lurked.

And tentacles. Tentacles everywhere.

They slithered between the figures, slid from beneath their robes, oozed from the open doorways.

Kenny screamed. "We're done for. Done for!"

"Oh, pull yourself together, man," Loretta snapped, slapping him across the face.

His yells stopped. Holding a hand to his face, nostrils flaring, he glared at Loretta. "*How* dare you?"

She rolled her eyes. "Outside, come on! Down the stairs."

They ran, and their sex mad chasers followed.

The Nookienomicon

The slithering tentacles shot out, seeking the group as they raced down the stairs. One snatched Jeff's ankle, tripping him.

"Oh, leave him," Kenny cried, charging away. "We'd be miles away by now if we hadn't gone looking for him."

"Leave me?" Jeff shouted, kicking the tentacle away as Loretta helped him to his feet. "Wait until I get my hands on you!"

"Now, boys," she yelled, almost losing her footing on the slick stairs. The place seemed to ooze slime all of a sudden. "We need to work... oh."

Kenny had reached the bottom of the stairs. Chastity had somehow got there first.

She stood, arms wide, tentacles extended from her stomach, smiling.

Kenny didn't stand a chance.

The slithering arms grabbed him, lifting him into the air, his bed sheet floating to the floor. They wrapped around his arms, his legs, his waist.

"NO!" he screamed, but the cry cut off as a tentacle slithered down his throat.

Kenny jerked. Chastity's eyes rolled back with pure pleasure. And the chants grew louder.

With a yank, the tentacles tore Kenny apart, gore showering the dank floor and walls of the Hotel Dagon, covering Chastity's pale skin, turning it crimson.

"Oh, bugger," Jeff muttered. "I was starting to like him. At least he left a woman satisfied before the end."

"Run!" Loretta sobbed, tears in her eyes. She actually *did* like Kenny. "We have to get out of

The Nookienomicon

here."

They raced by Kenny's shredded corpse to the hotel doors.

Locked.

They rattled as Jeff and Loretta shook them. Outside, thunder rolled and lightning flashed.

"What do we do now?" Jeff asked, grabbing Loretta's hand.

She turned. Chastity watched them. The robed figures approached, knives glinting, chants on their tongues.

Something on the floor caught her eye. The Nookinomicon.

Grabbing it, she clutched it to her chest, opened it, and read the first line she came across.

"Ph'nglui mglw'nafh," she yelled, the words feeling rough in her throat. The figures in black robes paused, though. "Cthulhu R'lyeh wgah'nagl fhtagn."

"Come again?" Jeff muttered.

Throwing the book aside, she threw herself at Jeff, locking her lips on his, wrapping her legs around his ever-tightening red Speedos.

"If you can't beat them, love," Loretta whispered, pulling her lips away. "Join 'em."

"Sex mad," Jeff laughed, running his hands over Loretta's body. "Bloody sex mad."

They fell to the floor, losing themselves in pleasure as the robed figures of the Hotel Dagon chanted their approval.

Loretta and Jeff never left the Hotel Dagon again. And nor did they want to.

VI

A Nasty Little Cult
by Callum Pearce

Tig hated being late. As she rushed down the street toward the coach that was going to take her and her fellow mature students on their field trip, she could see Professor Feeley was standing next to the open door of the coach. He was pointedly looking at his watch and then back to her. She quickened her pace and made her apologies when she arrived at the coach door.

"Ah, Miss Bitties, glad to see you could finally join us," Feeley leaned in a little too close to her as he spoke.

"Sorry I'm late. You wouldn't believe the morning I've had..." Tig began.

"Probably not. On you go, we haven't got all day."

As she rushed past him onto the coach, she felt his hand patting her backside. For a brief moment, she entertained the idea of turning around and snapping his wrinkly little fingers off. Instead, she giggled and rushed up the steps away from them. Dick was sat next to Roger in the middle of the coach, grinning at her. Well, more accurately grinning at her breasts as she rushed down the aisle. She saw that Anita was sitting alone behind them, so rushed to the seat next to her. She liked Anita. One of the quieter members of the group, unless you rubbed her up the wrong way. Anita had spent

The Nookienomicon

most of her adult life raising her sons and running around after her lazy husband. Then one day, the kids were grown up and her husband was off chasing skirt around the local bars. She'd always had an interest in ancient religions. When she finally had some time to herself, she joined Professor Feeley's course.

"Glad to see everyone made it." Professor Feeley stood at the front of the coach with Professor Shanks standing nervously beside him. "Some of us even managed to get here on time," he added, glaring at Tig. "Now, there's a reason I've chosen you, shall we say, more mature members of our class."

"Older maybe, not too sure about mature," Anita sneered, prodding the back of Dick's chair.

"Now this excursion is a very weighty affair. We're very lucky to have been allowed to visit such a relatively recent discovery," Feeley continued, ignoring Anita. "I want you all taking this very seriously. This isn't some school trip; you're not going to spend the journey canoodling at the back of the bus..."

"'Ere what's canoodling, Professor?" Tig asked innocently.

"Get to the back of the bus and I'll show you. Nyahahaha," Dick laughed, turning around to face them. He laughed like a dirty old man. There was a good reason for this - he *was* a dirty old man.

"Naughty," Tig giggled.

"You keep your noodle in your pants, Dick Trickle," Anita piped up. "Turn back around in your chair too. Your dog breath is steaming up my

135

The Nookienomicon

glasses."

Dick nudged Roger hard in the ribs when he turned back around in his seat, hoping to stop him giggling into his hands. Harry, who was sitting across the aisle from the women, smiled sweetly and rolled his eyes. Tig loved old Harry, he generally kept himself to himself but every so often would floor her with a perfect line or comeback. She genuinely never knew whether he meant to be funny or not. He was sweet and a bit camp. Harry acted very much like an innocent old lady but she was sure he had a good dose of filthy humour hiding beneath the surface. The professors Feeley and Shanks sat down at the front of the coach, suggesting that they had said all that they had to say for now. Tig knew when they arrived at their destination, they would be in for more lectures. It didn't matter that they were mature students. To Feeley's mind, everyone was beneath him, less mature, less knowledgeable, hardly worth his time.

Tig pulled out the novel she had been working her way through for the last week and Anita took out her knitting. Eventually, trying to concentrate on the words in the book and the gentle clicking from the seat next to her made her eyes feel heavy. She put her head against the window and drifted off to sleep.

Her dreams were strange and disjointed. One moment she was floating in the vast, soul-sucking vacuum of space. Her body remained together but she felt as though her memories and personality were being pulled in a million directions. For those moments, she felt as though she was living in a

The Nookienomicon

million bodies at once. She could remember lives she hadn't lived. She could smell the decaying corpses around her in wars she had never fought in. Before she could fully grasp any of the tendrils of these memories, she felt cold wet air hitting her in the face. When she closed her eyes, those memories were gone. She could almost feel them drifting away from her body like the frayed edges of a dream when you wake up. She wanted to reach out and grab them back. Opening her eyes, she found herself standing alone in a dark, cold cave. In front of her was a deep pit. There seemed to be splashes of blood against the rocks at the side. At the bottom of the pit, she could see what looked like large tentacles writhing and folding over each other. For a moment, there was a flash of a giant mouth filled with pointed teeth closing together as more tentacles slithered to cover it. Large, bloodshot eyes opened all along each tentacle and blinked at her.

"I have theen your final moment." The voice travelled up from the pit to Tig's ears. As terrified as she was, she still couldn't help but find the lisp distracting.

"I can already tathte your thacrifithe."

"Taste my what?" Tig gasped. The terror had already transformed into deep concentration as she tried to figure out what the voice was trying to tell her. "Oh, sacrifice?"

"The blood of your party will thummon me to the great featht,"

"Great feast?" Tig was getting the hang of this now.

"The end of the univerthe ath you know it," the

The Nookienomicon

voice lisped. "Chaoth, confuthion, conflicth."

Tig laughed out loud and then felt instantly guilty. She ran the words back through her head a couple of times until she had worked out what the voice had been trying to say. Concentrating so hard had made her miss the giant tentacle that was creeping up the side of the pit towards her. It dived up the last part quickly and wrapped around her waist and stomach, pushing her breasts up under her chin.

"The featht beginth with you," the voice roared.

"Let me go, this can't be real!" Tig shouted through her rising breasts.

"Tig!" Was that Anita's voice shouting in the distance? "Tig, wake up, we're there."

Tig felt the strength of the tentacles evaporate and her breasts flop back down where they belonged. Her eyes flicked open then she squinted to adjust to the daylight filling the coach.

"I must have dropped off," Tig mumbled.

"Dropped off? You've been snoring like an old sow for the last two hours," Dick laughed. He was standing in the aisle trying to get his overstuffed backpack out of the rack above his seat.

"There's only one dirty old swine on this bus, Dick, and it ain't me," Tig snapped. The dream was already leaving her, except for the image of the creature at the bottom of the pit. The tentacles still writhed and wriggled in her mind. The eyes still glared at her hungrily.

Dick gave his bag handle one last hard yank and claimed it back from the grasping rack. As the bag came loose, he stumbled back and fell heavily in

The Nookienomicon

Harry's lap.

"Oh, I say," Harry cackled. "You didn't even buy me a drink first." Dick jumped up red-faced and flustered.

"Hurry up you lot," Professor Feeley shouted from the front of the bus. "Come along Dick, you're holding everyone up."

Once Dick was out of the way, everyone else managed to get their things and exit the bus without any fuss. Professor Feeley stopped Tig on the steps. She was still giggling about the happy look of surprise on Harry's face when Dick had landed in his lap.

"This is a very serious exploration that we have been allowed to do here." Coffee, cigarettes and possibly whisky from the night before wafted into Tig's face as he leaned in and breathed his words at her. "I'd be very grateful if you could get your titters out here on the bus."

"You want me to do what? 'Ere you can't ask me to do that, you filthy beast." Tig knew exactly what he meant, but loved to watch his face puff up and glow bright red.

"I mean the laughter, the childish behaviour. I didn't mean... I would never..."

Tig pushed past him down the last few steps and off the stuffy, hot coach. She carried on tittering to herself until she joined the rest of the group. They all watched as Feeley and Shanks collected their cases and bags, bickering between themselves as they went about it. She was sure that Shanks hated having to put up with his irritating colleague. He was a terribly pompous thing. His nose would flare

The Nookienomicon

as he lectured you with his perfect diction and Rs rolling around all over the place. Only when Feeley was in the vicinity, his shoulders would stoop and his head would lower. Feeley would never let him forget who was in charge and who was only there to assist the great professor. Sometimes Tig would see Feeley watching Shanks get a bit above himself. He would give him just enough time to get to the height of haughtiness that would be the most fun to slap him down from. Then, he would swoop in and take him down several pegs in front of any audience that was around.

"Gather round everyone. Now, these caves have been made as safe as they possibly can be, but they are still caves. You all need to be alert at all times. We can't expect to make any great discoveries here today. The caves have already been thoroughly explored and all finds have been documented. What I expect you to do is follow the path of the previous explorers. Think about what methods you would use if you were the first to witness everything here," Professor Feeley droned on.

Tig found herself thinking about the tentacles and eyes from her dream. She imagined pushing through the caves to find the giant pit she had been standing over. She pictured that awful creature rolling about beneath her. She didn't need to listen to Feeley yammering on, he was only repeating what he had told them all in class the day before. The man just adored the sound of his own voice... ancient cults... blah blah blah... Gods from before time... blah blah blah.

"CONCENTRATION!" Professor Feeley

The Nookienomicon

shouted, dragging her back into the lecture.

"Bog Buggeroth was believed to be the progenitor of whom, Miss Bitties?"

"The Great Old One, Cthulhahoop, Professor Feeley," she droned back at him.

"Indeed, amongst others, but well done," Feeley grinned, his tobacco-stained teeth making her stomach turn.

"I think we should be getting on with things now," Professor Shanks mumbled.

"Who is in charge here?" Professor Feeley snapped.

"You are, of course, Professor. I would never dream of stepping on your ever so talented toes." Shanks was slithering more than the evil tentacles from Tig's dream.

"Right then guys and girls," Feeley declared, causing Tig to almost cringe herself inside out. "Let's go and see what we're here to see." He clapped his hands together and gave them all a smug grin. "Don't forget what I always say, teamwork makes the dream work."

Tig almost laughed in his face. A stolen line like all of his stolen discoveries. He wasn't nearly as well-known as he imagined himself to be. If he was known at all, it was for the many court cases when he had smeared himself over somebody else's discoveries and made them his own. It was guaranteed that if any of them found anything in these caves, Feeley would trample them to death in his rush to get to any waiting TV or news cameras. He would stamp his name all over anything and write long-winded, awful books about other

The Nookienomicon

people's work. He'd lived his whole life off his father's name and contacts. Any weight his name had, came from his father. Feeley senior was widely recognised as the expert in all things connected to the Nookienomicon. It was his work that had drawn Tig into this area of study in the first place. Feeley loved the recognition but hated the work. Tig had always thought that he would have been better suited as a gym teacher. Not because he was particularly active or sporty, just because she always imagined him with a whistle around his neck looking up women's skirts.

They entered the caves in single file, moving carefully around the scaffolding and wooden beams that had been set up, presumably for health and safety. Tig could see that Professor Feeley was already captivated by two large domes in the rock above him. Each had what Tig could only describe as nipples in the centre.

"Cor, that looks just like..." Professor Shanks gasped.

"A right lovely pear," Dick interrupted. Feeley spun around to admonish him until he saw that he was looking at a different rock that actually did look like a juicy pear hanging above them.

"Do you think?" Anita asked. "I think it looks more like a great big..."

"Balzak!" Feeley shouted. "Come away from there, don't touch."

Harry spun around, yanking his hand away from the wall with the bright green symbols he was just about to run his fingers over. Feeley rushed over, trailed by the rest of the group.

The Nookienomicon

"Have you all got the pamphlets I gave you?" Feeley asked the group. They all rummaged in their bags. They pulled out the stapled together pages of photos and text, all about the discoveries that were made when the caves had first been explored. "You'll find a photograph of this on page one. If you look here at the top," he ran his fingers over two of the symbols, "these are clearly the symbols for Bog Buggeroth. You see the eye there and the tentacles that come away. Next to it are the orbs that people believed were the form he would take when moving from one universe to the next. These symbols underneath seem a bit more worn..." He ran his fingers over the ones beneath the ancient creature's name.

"Erm, Professor, I don't think..." Shanks tried to interrupt.

"I don't think anyone could tell you what these mean in this state," Feeley continued.

"Excuse me, Professor," Shanks mumbled. "I think I might be able..."

"You can surely see I'm trying to teach these people something here," Feeley snapped. He ran his fingers over the symbols again. "This one here could possibly mean..."

"But Professor, I really think you should..."

"Not now, Professor Shanks. If I can't read them, I'm pretty sure you can't either. How many famous reports have been written by the great Armitage Shanks so far? Don't count on your fingers Balzak. None, that's how many."

There was a strange groaning noise and a crack started to appear in the wall next to Feeley's hand.

The Nookienomicon

The crack was filled with razor-sharp teeth. Behind those, where it should have been more rock, it looked like red, wet flesh. Feeley froze in shock long enough for the strange mouth to clamp down on his hand, slicing it clean off. The rest of the group stepped back together but Feeley stayed rooted to the spot, his blood spraying all over the wall. He was screaming in pain; the group watched in horror as he bent over, and the rock stretched out so that the mouth could close over his head. Tig wanted to close her eyes but couldn't. Feeley's headless body started to fall backwards. Tig was sure she could still hear the head screaming as it was swallowed by the wall. The sound of the body hitting the ground and the splashing blood woke everyone like a slap in the face.

They all turned and ran back to where they had entered the caves. The wooden frame that had surrounded the opening was still there, but it seemed as though the rock had grown around it. The only way out they knew of was gone as though it had never been there.

Anita screamed at the top of her lungs, then for want of a better idea screamed again and again. Shanks stepped forward and slapped her hard in the face. This caused the chain reaction of her arm sweeping up and slapping him hard in his. Harry was gulping from a hip flask he had pulled out of his bag.

"I'm sorry, but you were hysterical," Shanks explained.

"It is not HYSTERICAL to scream when you're trapped in a cave. Especially when you've just

The Nookienomicon

watched a man have his bloody head chomped off by a wall!" Anita shouted.

Shanks' nostrils flared as they often would before he launched into some pompous lecture. Tig could see that as deluded and self-important as he was, even he couldn't argue with what Anita had said.

"What did the symbols mean?" Dick asked, trying and failing to hide the tremble in his voice.

"It was a warning for the members of the cult of Bog Buggeroth," Shanks replied.

"Yeah, but what did it say?"

"I'm not completely certain, but it looked like *do not touch*," Shanks mumbled.

"Oof, he probably should have listened to you then," Harry laughed, taking another gulp from his flask.

"How can you laugh at a time like this?" Anita complained. "A man just died."

"Gin, dear," Harry replied. "And there's plenty more where that came from." He opened his bag to show that it was mostly full of the small flasks. "Want some?"

Harry waved the bottle under Anita's nose, but she turned away disgusted. Tig happily snatched it from him and took a big mouthful of the bitter liquid. Dick took it from her for his turn and then Roger helped himself. He passed it to Professor Shanks who turned it upside down to pour out what was left. Luckily, it was already finished off. Harry took the flask from him and swapped it for one of the full ones in his bag.

"Getting drunk isn't going to help any of us,"

The Nookienomicon

Shanks moaned.

"It's helping me already," Harry cackled. "Although that was my third flask and seeing two of you is not a pretty sight, I must say." He squinted defiantly at the professor and took a swig from the new flask. "Chin, chin."

They were distracted when the lights in the small chamber they occupied blinked out and a row of bright emergency lights flickered to life behind them. They illuminated a long, twisting tunnel. They were all clearly happy to see anything leading away from the place where Professor Feeley's body still lay, oozing blood onto the cold ground. Everyone pushed toward the new path with Shanks doing his best to elbow his way to the front. He had finally been given his chance to lead. Tig suspected he wasn't exactly cut up by the death of his colleague. He marched through the tunnel, looking around him as though the excursion was just going to carry on as usual.

"Listen now everyone, shh, listen!" Shanks put his arms out to stop them from moving. "You hear that sound?"

"Ooh, that's creepy, it's putting the willies right up me," Anita complained.

"Nyahaha," Dick laughed.

"It sounds like voices," Tig volunteered.

"Yeeeees," Shanks replied, dragging the word out too long and grinning from ear to ear. "It does, doesn't it? But it isn't actually. If you look at the top of the cave there, you can see small holes drilled and grooves chiselled into the rock, see. We believe that the old cults that used these caves would do this

The Nookienomicon

deliberately. They would have a central chamber where the ceremonies would be held, but the tunnels leading away from the main chamber would be filled with these. When the wind passed through the tunnels it would make the sound of soft singing. Really quite clever if you ask me. It was said that the music would call to people, luring them to the central chamber where they would be sacrificed."

"Clever old cults," Dick laughed.

"And we're just going to carry on going this way, are we? To the sacrifice chamber?" Anita asked.

"Nobody has practised Nookiemancy for centuries," Shanks explained as though he was talking to a child who was scared of the bogeyman. Not a grown woman who had just seen somebody eaten by a cave wall. "If we can hear the noise, then there must be wind coming from somewhere, you see?" He tapped his flared nostrils and grinned a terrible, smug grin.

"A way out!" Tig exclaimed.

"Precisely," Shanks said, nodding his big, smug head.

"'Ere, I hope we haven't got any virgins in this group," Harry cackled before swigging from his flask.

"Unlikely," Roger mumbled. "Although..." He pointed towards Shanks. Just a second too late, he changed the gesture to brushing his hair as Shanks' face snapped round to look at him.

"Wrong actually. It doesn't matter anyway," Shanks explained. "The cults allegedly preferred older people for the sacrifices. It was believed that when their blood was offered, Bog Buggeroth

The Nookienomicon

would also absorb their souls and their experiences." The group just stared at him. "Yeah, that's shut you up, hasn't it?" Shanks laughed as he spun around and started marching down the tunnel again.

The group followed him, looking and listening for any signs of danger. The eerie music that floated along the tunnels drew Tig back into her dream. She saw the monstrous mouth grinning up at her and the blinking eyes scanning her whole body.

Thacrifithe. She remembered the strange voice talking to her.

"Somebody grab one of the torches and aim it up that shaft," Shanks said. Dick already had a torch in his hand, so he turned it on and pointed it at the back of Shank's pants. "I'm not seeing anything, are you aiming it right up the shaft?"

"Oh, up there? I see what you mean," Dick laughed as he stopped shining the torch at the professor's backside and up to a small shaft that had been cut out above them.

"I knew it!" Shanks exclaimed. "See that symbol there, at the top?"

Everyone looked up the shaft to a large glowing symbol at the end of it. Tig found it hard to focus as it seemed to squirm and writhe as she stared at it. It must have been a trick of the light, but it made her quite queasy.

"This wasn't just a place of worship and sacrifices!" Shanks was clearly getting excited. "This is leading to a summoning chamber. There will be five of these tunnels leading from one central chamber. Five people would be sacrificed,

The Nookienomicon

and they believed each of their souls would lead Bog Buggeroth's tentacles down one of the tunnels out into the world. The eyes would take in the new world as his body slowly rose from the pit."

"And he had five of them, did he?" Dick asked, Shanks nodding excitedly. "Must have been a bugger to cross his legs."

"TEN...ta...cles." Shanks was losing patience with Dick's attitude. "But I think you knew that already, didn't you?" Dick and Roger laughed at the professor's irritation. Harry giggled, hiccupped and farted then took another swig from his gin.

"There could be people waiting here now," Tig suggested. "Hoping to restart the religion. Waiting to feed souls to some tentacled monster. Our souls."

"I bet you won't call them that to their faces," Dick laughed.

"Call them what? Oh, oops," Tig giggled. "Cheeky."

"Ooh, I'm coming over all queer," Harry said, staggering backwards a couple of steps. Tig was sure Dick must have bitten right through his tongue trying not to comment on that line.

"Too much of this, I suspect," Anita snapped, grabbing the flask from Harry's hand. She was obviously getting annoyed with the whole situation.

"Something's coming all over me," Harry moaned, pulling at his shirt buttons, trying to open it. Tig could see Dick straining not to make a childish comment.

When Harry opened his shirt, everyone gasped as his skin started to crack. Symbols appeared over his chest, neck and face as though cut into him by an

The Nookienomicon

invisible knife. Professor Shanks rushed over to him and opened his shirt fully to get a better look at the symbols. Anita passed the flask of gin back to Harry without thinking. He opened and drank from it in much the same manner.

"Does it hurt?" Tig asked.

"It just feels like loads of little pricks all over my body," Harry replied. This was too much for Dick, he guffawed loudly right into Harry's frightened face. Anita clipped him around the ear. She gave him a look that suggested he think very carefully about what he said or did next.

"Does it mean anything?" Tig asked Professor Shanks.

"I think this part on his chest says something like, the sixth shall tell the tale," Shanks explained. "The rest seem unfinished but here on his left shoulder it looks like the word for teacher, the other side looks like mother."

"It's us, isn't it?" Anita interrupted. "It's our tales, we're going to be the five sacrifices."

They had all begun to suspect it. Someone saying the words out loud made the realisation hit them like a brick to the face. There was no way out back the way they had come. They had no choice but to carry on pushing forwards along the tunnel. Now, every step felt heavier, and even Dick seemed solemn as they all trudged onward. The eerie music continued to flow around them like a siren's song. Thankfully, Harry was happy to keep passing the flasks around. Nobody turned their noses up this time. As the gin warmed their throats and clouded their minds, another sound rose above the music of

The Nookienomicon

the tunnels. A distant chanting that they continued to walk towards as though sleepwalking. Even if there had been a way out behind them, the group were moving on autopilot now. They were all lost in the dreams that the chanting was pushing into their minds.

Tig imagined she was standing on a beach. She heard the frantic cries of people that ran past her and the screeching of seagulls above. Giant tentacles rose above the water, humanoid creatures chased the people. Their mouths were massive, splitting their giant heads in two. Their sharp gnashing teeth reminded her of the mouth in the cave wall. Even though everybody was running in the opposite direction, Tig continued to walk forward towards the monsters that filled the sea. She didn't feel scared, she didn't feel much at all except for the damp air that caressed her face and body. A giant, hideous head rose from the water, the mouth from her dream opened in the middle of it. Eyes flicked open all over its face and glared at her.

"Finally, we featht," the creature lisped. The thing spoke quietly but the words drifted effortlessly over waves and into her head. "Your thoul will lead me back to your univerthe. I can almost tathte your blood." Its mouth opened wide as it seemed to inhale the salt air around it.

Tig continued to walk into the water, staring at the creature. A voice deep inside her was screaming to turn back, but to no avail. She continued to wade deeper into the dark water, staring at the thing in front of her until her head slipped beneath the waves. The saltwater stung so she closed her eyes.

The Nookienomicon

The sounds had all stopped now, for a moment, until she started to hear the chanting again.

When she opened her eyes, she was standing with the rest of her group in a large open chamber. In the centre, was a wide, deep pit like the one from her dream, with five wooden posts placed around the edges. The others looked as though they were just waking up themselves. Seven hooded figures walked slowly out of the tunnels around the place. The chanting seemed to be coming from beneath their hoods. One of them raised their hand and all of them stopped chanting at once. Tig was baffled, she was sure they couldn't see him without pulling their hoods back a bit. The one who had held his hand up walked towards their group. He held a small staff with a big, sharp blade crammed into the end. She noticed now that the others were holding small daggers with intricately carved handles. He waved the staff in front of him.

"Don't you waggle your stick in my face," Anita snapped, irritation overcoming the fear for just a moment.

"Call the priestess," the man in front of them shouted without looking back to the others. One of them pulled a large horn from somewhere in their long robes. They put the end under their hood and blew hard. The sound filled the chamber for a moment and then silence returned.

Nobody dared to move with the man holding his weapon out in front of them. Tig noticed somebody moving along the central tunnel toward the chamber. She soon saw that it was a beautiful woman. Jet black hair fell around her shoulders, her

The Nookienomicon

skin was as white as chalk and her lips as red as blood. Her long black dress revealed just enough of her breasts to make even Tig feel a little jealous. If you wanted to draw the perfect shaped woman, this is who you would draw.

"Finally, someone has given me the horn." Her husky voice floated from her like a long sigh. "I could have slept for at least another decade."

She seemed to glide toward them with her long dress trailing on the floor behind her. The men seemed mesmerised by her, even Harry couldn't seem to take his eyes off her. Tig looked from one to the other, hoping that someone would spring into action. She wracked her brain, trying to think of anything she could do. Nobody moved and no ideas presented themselves.

"Oh, what absolute darlings," the priestess sighed. "Ah, my storyteller." She was looking at the symbols carved into Harry's body. She held out her hand and Harry stepped forward to take it in his. "My boys will take you in hand, dear fellow." A couple of the hooded figures moved forward and led Harry to a large, raised slab of rock near the tunnel the priestess had emerged from. "New pages for the Nookienomicon, remove them carefully boys."

Tig was horrified to see that Harry didn't put up a fight at all. He allowed them to lead him to the slab where he lay down calmly. The two cultists raised their knives and went to work, carefully removing a large patch of skin from his chest. She tried to rush forward but the hooded man held his weapon out in front of her.

"Ooh, you all want a piece of me, don't you?

The Nookienomicon

Naughty boys," she heard Harry saying as the men continued their gruesome task.

"Now listen here, do you know who I am?" Shanks started.

"Professor Armitage Shanks," the man with the staff replied. Shanks looked quite pleased to have been recognised. "I'm a little disappointed, to be honest, I was hoping I would get to see Feeley die." He pulled back his hood and grinned at Shanks. What had previously been an intimidating presence was now just a frumpy old man in an oversized cloak.

"It never is? Paddy Cake!" Shanks gasped.

"Professor Cake, if you don't mind, or High Priest Cake will do."

"He was a colleague of Professor Feeley's," Shanks whispered to the group.

"That man took everything from me. He stole my work and published it as his own," Cake began. "I was a naive young man, placing his trust in a more experienced colleague. That man stole my innocence."

"I don't think he quite went that far," Shanks snorted.

"You know what I mean. I trusted people, I believed in people until that man..."

As he ranted and whined, he lowered the staff to better enjoy his self-pity party and Tig saw her opportunity. She kicked him hard between the legs. When she did, all the men in the room, including the cultists in their robes, crossed their legs and groaned in sympathy. Then, Tig threw herself forward, forcing the whining professor back

The Nookienomicon

towards the large pit. He tried to grab at her as he fell backwards but she managed to pull away just in time. His screams carried on for a long time as he disappeared into the darkness. She listened for the satisfying crunching or splashing sound that would let her know his body had found the bottom, but it never came. She was glad not to see the beast from her dreams lurking down there waiting for her. She had expected to turn around to see the others wrestling with the priestess or the other cult members but instead, they all stood still staring at the priestesses outstretched hand.

"Come on then you lot, get her," Tig shouted to the group.

"I'm afraid they're quite incapable of movement dear, as are you," the priestess said.

As soon as she said the words, Tig's legs felt too heavy to move, her whole body froze, only her eyes flicked from side to side.

"Now let's get things started, shall we?" the priestess said softly. "You there. You may step forward." She pointed to Roger. He walked slowly toward her. "And what is your name, you big hunk of a man?"

"Rogers, ma'am," Roger replied. "Roger R. Rogers,"

"Out of interest, what does the R stand for? Surely not..." she laughed.

"Roger, ma'am," Roger replied.

"Roger Roger Rogers, oh my word," she giggled. "Your parents must have had a wonderful sense of humour or simply no imagination at all. Follow me."

The Nookienomicon

She turned around and moved towards the first post, Roger following obediently. When she moved, Tig could see tentacles peeping out from under her long, black dress.

"Stand by that post," she insisted.

"Don't think I'll bother, if you don't mind," Roger replied.

"You what?" The priestess looked at him puzzled. "Nobody can resist me, do as you're told." A large tentacle whipped out from under her dress and wrapped around Roger's arms and chest. Tig heard gasps coming from under the cultist's hoods.

"How can you resist me?" she asked.

"Oh, you're not really my type," Roger said, matter of factly. "All tits and tentacles, no thank you."

"You know I could pop your head off right where you stand without making a scrap of effort?" she warned.

"I thought you need all of us for the summoning," Roger reminded her.

"You don't think I could find a volunteer to replace you?" She gestured to the cultists that were standing together. "Any one of those would step forward in a second." The cultists all stepped back as one. "Cowards!" Another tentacle whipped out to move Roger over to the first post.

"Bugger this," mumbled a voice from under one of the hoods. Then, the ones standing together all turned and ran down one of the tunnels. The two that had been working on Harry turned round to see the priestess with her tentacles out, her eyes now glowing red. Seeing their friends disappearing in the

The Nookienomicon

distance lit a fire under them. They both stumbled over each other to get out of there. It occurred to Tig that they must have been some of Cake's bored, old colleagues. Out for a bit of fun and games, playing at being in a cult. They probably never imagined encountering any real monsters.

Tig could feel some movement coming back to her. Slowly, her muscles were untightening, the creature's power over her fading. The priestess's tentacles were moving fast, tying Roger to the post. Tig could see that the others were starting to move their heads a little. She noticed that the High Priest's staff had fallen next to the pit before he had taken his unfortunate tumble over the edge. Tig willed Roger to keep the priestess distracted. She didn't need to will it at all. For a quiet man, Roger seemed quite happy for the chance of a good chat today.

"Not much use of a priestess with no followers," he teased. "Do things like you really have any power without the faith of your flock?"

"Things like me!" she shouted. "You know nothing of me and my kind. We roamed this planet when it was an empty rock, and we will take it back to those times again with my king at my side."

"But I thought old Buggeroth loved a bit of chaos," Roger continued. "Won't be getting much of that on an empty planet."

"Your mind is so small," she screamed. "We have all of time and space to play in. Your planet is a mere hors d'oeuvres."

"Ooh I've never been a fan of them horses doovers, way too fiddly and faffy," Roger complained. "I'm more a meat and two veg man

The Nookienomicon

myself."

Dick's sudden laughter could have ruined the moment as the priestess spun to look at him. Luckily, Tig was already behind her, holding the staff in front. She pushed the blade deep into the creature's back and shoved her toward the pit. The priestess screamed a mind-numbing, high-pitched scream as the rest of the group rushed over to help Tig.

The human half of the priestess seemed to fold back into a rapidly swelling green, slimy blob that was bubbling up from under her dress. Eyes opened all over the thing, tentacles whipped around trying to grab at the group. Dick punched it hard in one of the eyes, Anita took her shoe off and set about it with that. Even Shanks was kicking and punching any part of the thing that came near him. The thing slipped over into the pit but hung on to the edge with its tentacles. Tig stabbed at them with the blade in the staff and jumped on the ones she wasn't stabbing. Dick grabbed a knife from the slab where they had been working on Harry. He returned and began stabbing and slicing at the limbs that gripped the edge of the pit. As the thing gave up under the relentless attack, it tried to grab at Tig to take her down with it. She moved quickly out of the way, so the thing only managed to grab hold of her clothes. She felt her bra straps twanging open as the creature disappeared into the pit, carrying her bra and T-shirt with it.

"Cor blimey!" Dick exclaimed. He looked like he was about to start stamping his foot like a randy rabbit.

The Nookienomicon

"Miss titties... I mean Bitties. Put them away." Shanks frantically removed his jacket and rushed over to cover Tig's body up as quickly as possible.

When she was suitably covered, she used the blade on the staff to cut the ropes holding Roger to the post. They all rushed over to Harry. He was lying on the slab with a happy little smile on his face. Tig felt like vomiting when she saw the exposed flesh on his chest where his skin had been removed. Harry didn't seem bothered by it at all. He sat up and reached down next to the slab where his flask of gin had fallen. The others just stared at his chest in horror as he happily took a long, well-deserved gulp. When he noticed the others looking, he looked down at his chest too.

"Ooh, that's going to hurt in the morning," he chuckled, taking another swig of gin.

Some of the group helped him to his feet and they started moving to one of the tunnels. Tig went back to the pit first to make sure nothing was making its way up the side. The pit was dark and silent; she threw the staff over the edge and followed the group along the tunnel. It was only when the fresh air hit them outside, that Tig truly felt like the ordeal was over. Only then did her brain start to process everything that had happened.

"Thith wath not your time," the voice from her dream rose above her thoughts. "I thee all of time and thpace. One day, you will return, my thweet thacrifithe."

She didn't have time to dwell on the strange message as Dick and Anita were already bickering about which way to go to find the coach. Shanks

The Nookienomicon

was trying to shout over them and assert some authority. Roger was looking at her with concern, but simply smiled when she made eye contact. She joined the group and joined the argument. The real world was finally taking over the nightmare.

VII

The Search for Rhum'pee-Phum'pee
by Tim Mendees

Gropeham University, London, England, 1973.

Emma pulled the hem of her sky-blue polyester jersey over the waistline of the brown cords that she had pinched from her roommate. Her breath was ragged, coming in hesitant gasps as she hurried along the wood-panelled corridors of Gropeham University. Students milled around in whispering groups like furtive insects as she whisked past them without so much as acknowledging their existence.

"Come on, Emma, pull yourself together," she whispered as she came to a stop outside of her destination. She balled her fist and prepared to knock on the stout oak door with the gleaming brass nameplate reading 'Dr R Blocker. BSC'. Before her knuckles could make contact with polished wood, she hesitated, pulling her hand back like it had been stung.

It was strange for Emma to be so nervous. She was usually firm and resolute, but something about the head of the Archaeology department put the wind up her, and no mistake. Perhaps it was his snide tones and withering glances, but he made her feel about as tall as an ant. As a mature undergraduate, Emma had never once before been summoned to his office, so why now? What had she done that was so terrible to warrant a dressing down

The Nookienomicon

from the dreaded Doctor Roger Blocker?

Taking a deep breath, she gently rapped the door. No answer.

Emma leaned close to the door in an attempt to hear any movement. There was none. She tried again, a little harder.

"This is why we need knockers!"

"I beg your pardon?" Emma gasped as she spun around and peered into the fresh face of one of the junior professors.

Professor Cockett grinned disarmingly. He was a gangly fellow in his mid-thirties with a mop of unruly hair and a reputation as the clumsiest man on campus. "I've been saying for months that we should fit them all with knockers." He indicated the door. "You'll have to knock louder than that if you want old Blocker's attention. He's completely oblivious when he's in a brown study."

Emma tried to hide her relief. "Oh... I didn't realise he was busy. I'll come back later." As she turned to leave, the sound of flushing water made her stop in her tracks.

Cockett's grin widened. "You're alright. I think he's finished. Go on then, give him a good banging!"

"What?" Emma snapped, her face contorting with prudish shock.

Cockett indicated the door with a sideways nod.

"Oh, I see." Emma tittered. "Thank you, Professor Cockett, I will."

Cockett turned, muttering "rather you than me" under his breath and collided with a trio of first-year student girls. Papers, books and bodies were sent

The Nookienomicon

tumbling to the floor in an untidy heap.

Emma stifled a giggle and slammed her fist thrice into Blocker's door.

In a heartbeat, the door flew open, and the face of Dr Blocker appeared, his nostrils flaring with irritation. "Yes, yes. What is it? I'm not deaf, you know?"

"Oh, I'm sorry, Doctor Blocker," Emma gabbled, gesturing towards the tangle of limbs behind her. "Professor Cockett said to give you a good bang!"

"Oh!" Blocker exclaimed, watching Cockett try to extract his head from under a Laura Ashley dress. "The filthy beast! I don't have time for any of that nonsense. I have important work to do. Good day!"

Confused, Emma stopped Doctor Blocker shutting his door with her hand. "You wanted to see me, Doctor?"

"I did?" He looked her up and down. Finally, realisation dawned. "I did. Come in and stop messin' about... take a seat." Blocker strutted towards his desk with his scrawny chest puffed out and his buttocks clenched before sitting himself down with his legs crossed and his hands on his topmost knee.

Emma shut the door behind her and sat in the chair opposite. "What did you want to see me for, Doctor?" she asked, putting on her 'posh' voice and doing her best to bury her cockney twang.

"It has come to my attention, Miss Rhoyds, that your work has been slipping of late."

"It has?"

"It has, and it is my duty as head of the department to get to the bottom of what might be

The Nookienomicon

the problem."

Emma squirmed in her seat. The trousers she had borrowed from Vee were far too tight for her.

Blocker indicated the University crest on the wall behind his desk. "Here at Gropeham University, we pride ourselves on being receptive to our students' needs. Hence our motto, *tu es in manibus*. You are in safe hands." Blocker beamed with pride as Emma studied the crest with a look of bemusement. The centre of it depicted two large shields side-by-side with a hand cupping the bottom of each...

"Um. I didn't realise there was a problem with my work, Doctor."

"Really?" Blocker leaned forward, his eyebrow cocked. "Then how do you explain the fiasco with the Goosing Gorge skeleton the other morning?"

Emma blushed. She had been doing her best to forget about that regrettable incident. "How was I to know that the extra bone came from a separate specimen?" Pouting petulantly, she folded her arms over her chest.

"But why didn't you ask your professor before fixing it where you did?"

"It seemed like a logical place for it to go!"

Blocker gasped. His mouth formed a perfect O. After a moment, he composed himself. "It is clear to me that you are, how shall I put it, distracted of late. Take a look at these sketches."

"What are they?" Emma asked haughtily.

"They are your anatomical sketches of what you think the Goosing Gorge Man would look like."

Emma reviewed her drawings. The figure was

The Nookienomicon

bipedal but hunched with elongated arms and a dog-like skull. "I don't see what the problem is. The skull has definite canine attributes."

"I'm not talking about its head, Miss Rhoyds. I'm referring to lower down." Blocker jabbed a bony finger towards the groinal area. "It's grossly exaggerated. Poor Professor Stiff in the anthropology department nearly had to change his classification from *Homo Canis* to *Homo Erectus Gigantis*!"

Under her tight blonde curls, Emma had turned as red as a beetroot. "I'm sorry, Doctor. I don't know what's come over me. I've been having these dreams, see?"

"Dreams?" Blocker raised an eyebrow.

"Yeah, every night."

"What about?"

"Well, erm..." She trailed off, her nerves getting the better of her.

"Come on, you can tell me. I've been trained to deal with all manner of..."

"Tentacles!" Emma's hand shot up towards her mouth but wasn't quick enough to stop the word from blurting out at extreme volume.

"Whaaat?" Blocker gasped. "Outrageous! That a girl from a good family should be having those sorts of dreams... it's disgusting!"

"Eh?" Emma gasped in response. "I don't see what's so disgusting."

"Dreaming about men's..."

"No!" She yelped, her voice going high and shrill enough to cut glass. "Tentacles, Doctor. Like a squid."

The Nookienomicon

"Oh... yes. I see." Blocker coughed nervously and straightened his tie before deciding to cover his mistake. "And it's disgusting! Foul, slippery things. Can't stand the creatures." He paused to take a sip of water before continuing his line of questioning. "Did anything happen to bring on these dreams? A trip to the aquarium, or bad sushi, perhaps?"

"Well..." Emma shifted uncomfortably in her seat, desperately wishing she had worn her usual slacks. "The first time was after Doctor Romper..." She trailed off distractedly.

Blocker bristled at the mention of his academic rival. If he'd leant any further over the desk, he'd have been lying on it. "Go on. Doctor Romper did what, exactly?"

"Well... One night after everyone else had gone..."

"Yes?" Blocker was salivating. This might be the juicy titbit he'd been waiting for to finally get Richard Romper removed from campus.

"He showed it to me." Emma's shoulders heaved as she finally unburdened herself.

Blocker gasped.

"He just pulled it out and plonked it on the workbench!"

"Then what?"

"Then, he gave me a pair of rubber gloves and told me to be gentle!"

"Right, that's it!" Blocker launched into a flurry of activity, scribbling on a notebook and reaching for his black Bakelite telephone. "He's gone too far this time. The board will have to listen to me now."

As he started to dial, Emma cried out. "Oh,

The Nookienomicon

Doctor Blocker, why did he show me the Nookienomicon?"

Blocker's finger was almost to the top of the last number. He stopped, letting the dial slowly tick back to its starting point, and replaced the receiver, disappointed. "He showed you the Nookienomicon?"

"Yes, Doctor. It was ghastly! The things... the positions... the tentacles!" Emma sobbed.

Deflated, Blocker waved his hand. "I'm sure no lasting harm has been done. I have it on good authority that Doctor Romper's big discovery is nothing more than an elaborate hoax. Now, run along. I'm sure you have work to be getting on with?"

Emma bristled, put out that, after finally telling someone about her nocturnal disturbances, she was being brushed off. "But, the dreams, Doctor?"

"Oh. I'm sure they are nothing to worry about." He waved his hand again, more interested in what he was scribbling on his notepad. "I recommend a cold shower morning and night and eat plenty of roughage. Healthy bowel, healthy mind, that's what I always say."

"Um. Yes, Doctor." Emma shrugged, forced a smile, and raced for the door. As she pulled it open, she collided with a short, dishevelled man waving a brown paper bag. Emma let out a shriek of surprise that sounded akin to a startled moggie.

"I've got it!" the man announced. "I've got it!"

"Well, I don't want it, thank you very much!" Emma snarled, barging him aside.

The man huffed and dithered before focusing on

The Nookienomicon

Emma's too-tight cords as she marched away. A wistful smile spread across his haggard features.

"Professor Stroker!" Blocker snapped, shaking him from his reverie. "I hope you have a good reason for barging in here?"

"Yes, yes, I do." Stroker beamed, waving his package and slamming it onto the desk. "You were right, Doctor. Those fellows at Bona Books had it!"

"I knew it. They certainly looked the sort." Blocker's face lit up, elated. "And you managed to persuade them to give it to you?"

Stroker looked around to see that nobody was listening. Despite them being alone, he lowered his voice to a barely audible whisper. "The trouble was stopping them from trying to give it to me."

Blocker's nose looked like two railway arches as he gasped in shock. "The book, you fool!"

"Oh, yes," Stroker muttered, fishing in his pocket for the receipt. "Mr Sandy said it was nice to meet a man with an artistic bent. They gave me an invitation to pass on to you. Here..."

Blocker took the proffered card and the receipt. The card was pink with gold lettering. "Julien and Sandy invite you to their dolly cottage. Hmm. It must be an intellectual salon or something. Pity I'm so busy. I do miss the thrust of a good debate."

Stroker bit his lip and looked at the ceiling.

"Well, come on then, get it out!" Blocker demanded, startling Stroker.

"Eh?"

"The book, you bonehead!"

"Ah." Stroker picked up the package and slid it out from its brown paper bag. "There you go,

The Nookienomicon

Doctor. One copy of *Feeley's Notes on the Nookienomicon*."

"Oh, Willie, I could kiss you!" Blocker leapt from his seat and grabbed the tatty dog-eared volume. "You know what this means?"

"Um..."

"It means, my faithful colleague, that I will finally be able to prove that Romper's discovery is a fraud. He'll be ruined, you hear me... ruined!"

***

Doctor Roger Blocker strode into the main workshop of the Archaeology department with *Feeley's Notes...* under one arm and with Professor William Stroker following along behind like a loyal puppy. He paused in the centre of the room and scanned around for his prey. His eyes finally settled on a large projector screen. It was jiggling around like mad.

As the two men in tweed approached slowly, a girl's voice cried out. "Oh!"

"No, no, no," a man replied. "Hold it with both hands."

"It's too big!" the girl retorted.

Blocker's mouth once again became a big O for 'outrage'.

"Stop waving it around. You'll bend it." The man raised his voice in concern. "Right, that's better. Now, give it a good tug."

"Doctor Romper!" Blocker exploded. "Come out here this instant!"

The shock of his voice made both parties behind

The Nookienomicon

the screen yelp in surprise. There was a screech of metal followed by a loud rip as the leg of a lighting tripod burst through the silk.

"What're you playing at, you big nit? Now, look what you've done!" The man, Doctor Richard Romper, growled as he came out from behind the screen with a petite blonde in tow. "Oh, it's you, Doctor Blocker. What brings you down from your castle?" Blocker's plush office was on the second floor overlooking the fountain while Romper and the rest of the department were tucked away down in the basement.

The blonde, Emma's roommate, Vee, trotted in front of Doctor Romper. "Oh, Rick, I am sorry. What a clumsy little thing I am."

"Not so little." Rick grinned wolfishly, eyeing her tight sweater. He suddenly realised that Doctor Blocker was eyeing him with displeasure and quickly checked himself. "Erm. Not to worry, Miss Goodthyme, accidents happen. Go and help Professor Cockett load the shovels."

"Right you are." Vee giggled and wiggled off across the room. Stroker and Romper became instantly hypnotised by her hot pants that had to be at least a size too small. Until Blocker dug Stroker in the ribs with the point of his elbow, that is.

"If I can have your attention, please, gentlemen," Blocker sneered.

"Um. What?" Rick shook his head from side to side. "Yes, Doctor Blocker, what can I do for you?" Still, despite his best efforts, he couldn't resist another glance. "Phwoar!"

Blocker rolled his eyes. "Hold on one minute,

The Nookienomicon

Did you say Cockett?"

"Something along those lines. Wuhahaha!" Rick's craggy face crumpled into a mass of laughter lines as he chuckled heartily, nudging and winking at Stroker, who did his best to remain stone-faced.

Blocker huffed. "What is Professor Cockett doing down here?"

"Making a bleedin' mess most of the time." Rick chuckled again.

Almost on cue, a stack of shovels clattered to the floor as Cockett and Vee collided with them and ended up rolling around in a heap.

Blocker huffed again, his voice becoming nasal and whiny. "I mean, why isn't he up in the Theology department where he belongs?"

"What, 'aven't you 'eard?" Rick shrugged. "The Dean has given him to me on loan. He's coming with us on the dig tomorrow."

"Dig? What dig?" Blocker spat each word like it was poison.

"The dig over in Goosing Gorge. What do you think all this lot is for, a picnic?" Rick chuckled and indicated stacks of camping and archaeological equipment.

"Why haven't I been told about this?" Blocker fumed. "As the head of this department, I am to be consulted on any and all activities. Isn't that right, Stroker?"

Stroker nodded along with his colleague. "Except anything to do with the Nookienomicon."

Blocker kept nodding with a smug grin plastered across his face before the penny dropped, and he noticed what his toady had said. "What?"

171

The Nookienomicon

"You said that you didn't want to be bothered with Romper's nonsense and that he should take it up with the Dean," Stroker answered, scratching his chin as he tried to remember Blocker's exact words.

"What, I?" Blocker was flustered. He fiddled with his collar and tried to avoid looking Romper in the eye.

"You said," Stroker continued, "that you had important research to do and you didn't have time to chase wild geese with a second-rate archaeologist that wouldn't know a bonafide artefact if it slapped him in the face."

"Well... Um... I didn't use those exact words." Blocker wanted the ground to open up and swallow him.

"Yes, you did," Stroker asserted. "You told me to tell him to sling his hook and that if he wanted any money, he should ask the Dean personally as he wasn't getting a single penny out of you!"

"So that's what I did." Rick grinned. "He was more than happy to fund my expedition."

"This is an outrage!" Blocker's embarrassment had quickly morphed into unbridled rage. "You may have the Dean fooled, but I know your game. Your so-called Nookienomicon is nothing but a fake! And, I have the proof." He whipped out his copy of *Feeley's Notes...* and waved them under Rick's nose triumphantly.

Rick snatched the volume. "What's this?"

"It's the notes Professor Feeley Senior made when he examined pages from the real Nookienomicon. The transcripts in here will prove that yours is about as authentic as Japanese Scotch!"

The Nookienomicon

"Ta!" Rick grinned before tossing it onto a pile of camping equipment. "We're going to need some bog roll. Now, is there anything else?"

Blocker was apoplectic. "You haven't heard the last of this, Romper! You'll rue the day you crossed Doctor Roger Blocker!" As he fumed and raged, Rick gave another chuckle and sauntered off towards Cockett and Vee.

"Calm yourself, Doctor," Stroker simpered.

"Oh, he'll be sorry, mark my words." Blocker finally exhaled and straightened his tie. "Well, two can play at this game..." Without another word, he snatched up the copy of *Feeley's Notes...* and left.

Stroker rolled his eyes, took one last wistfully appreciative glance at Vee, then followed his colleague through the double doors.

***

Rick grinned as he admired the fabulous globes in front of him. "Blimey... I bet you don't get many of them to the pound!"

"What do you want?"

"Gimmie the pair." Rick rubbed his hands together and licked his lips.

"H... Huh 'ear... 'ear you go, Rick."

"Thanks, Charlie. I'm always partial to a fresh artichoke."

The man opposite Rick was tall, bespectacled, and wearing a flat cap, which was odd considering Charlie was a cook. Most people expected their cooks to wear white floppy hats, but not Charlie. In all his years at Gropeham, not one person had seen

The Nookienomicon

the top of his head. The dungarees he wore under his white coat simply added to the confusion. As Rick eyed the next tray of food in the makeshift canteen hungrily, Charlie did his best to get his nervous twitch under control.

"'Ere, Rick?" the musical voice of Vee called out from further down the lunch queue.

"Oops, sorry, Charlie, duty calls." Rick apologised as he cut the line, leaving the open-mouthed cook holding a jumbo sausage in a pair of metal tongs. "Yes, Vee, what can I do for you? Plenty, I hope? Wuhahaha!"

"Oh, saucy!" Vee giggled. "No. Me an' the girls were chatting and were wonderin' why the 'ell we have come all the way to Cornwall just to look at some old bones? There are plenty of bones on campus, and, I mean, when you've seen one bone, you've seen 'em all, right?"

"Well, that's not actually the case, you see, some are..."

Before Rick could finish his reply, a sausage was thrust between the pair. "Jumbo?"

Quick as lightning, Rick chuckled. "I've never had any complaints."

Vee also broke into hysterics and gave him a coy wink. "I'll bet."

"Thank you, Charlie." Rick nodded, accepting the sausage. Once it was safely wedged between two sumptuous domes of mashed spud, Rick turned Vee away from the rest of the line and lowered his voice. "It's not just bones we're out here for. That's just what I told the Dean. We are also out here looking for Rhum'pee-Phum'pee!"

The Nookienomicon

"Well, I know that." Vee gave him a playful nudge.

Rick looked around self-consciously. "No, the tomb of Rhum'pee-Phum'pee, the Hyperborean nookiemancer that first transcribed the Nookienomicon."

"Oh, I see." Vee chuckled. "It's easy to get the two mixed up, isn't it?"

"There will be plenty of time for that later," Rick leered.

"Oh!" Vee gasped, fluttering her long lashes. "Promises, promises. Just one thing though, if this Rumpy-Pumpy bloke was Hyperborean, why aren't we in Scotland?"

"Eh?"

"Well, my dad does the pools, and I 'eard that Hyperborea drew nil-nil with Partick Thistle on Saturday. It was a home game, and the man on the radio said it was in Edinburgh."

Rick shook his head. "No, no, no, that's..." Before he could correct her, a commotion broke out at the back of the lunch line. Bodies were being jostled and shoved forcefully aside. Someone was perpetuating the worst possible sin you could commit in Britain... queue jumping. "What the bloomin' 'ell is going on back there?"

Eventually, the source of the disturbance revealed itself. Vee gasped in horror. "Crikey, it's Doctor Blocker!"

"Damn, what the 'ell is he doing here?"

Blocker, and the ever-present Stroker, stopped and pointed a battered umbrella at Rick. "Ah, there you are, Romper. I want a word with you." He

The Nookienomicon

looked furious. Both he and Stroker were caked in mud from head to toe.

"Quick, get out of here, and not a word about Rhum'pee-Phum'pee," Rick hissed under his breath as Blocker weaved towards him, upending people's lunch trays.

"Or the Scottish bloke?"

"Or the Scottish bloke." Rick nodded. "Go on, go."

Vee turned sharply and collided with Doctor Blocker, tray first. It became wedged between his chest and hers, pushing up her assets so much that he couldn't help but stare at them.

"Fancy a portion?" Charlie asked, holding a scoop of mash.

"What? How dare you?" Blocker turned and hissed with such venom that poor Charlie's tick went into overdrive. He yelped, spun and flicked his arm. A dollop of creamy mash flew across the tent and landed directly in a brunette undergraduate's cleavage. She shrieked and leapt from her seat, snatching a dishcloth off a bewildered-looking elderly dinner lady. Vee used the ensuing pandemonium to extract herself from Blocker and make her escape. Stroker couldn't pass up an opportunity like this and started making a beeline for the distressed student.

"'Ere, where are you going?" Blocker called out after him.

Stroker stopped and bumbled for a second. "Erm. I'm just going to see if she needs any help." Puffing and panting, he fled across the tent.

"I don't fancy his chances, do you?" Rick

The Nookienomicon

chuckled, nudging Blocker with his elbow. "He'd be better off making a move on the dinner lady."

Within seconds of Stroker opening his mouth, there was a thunderous slap across his cheek that sent him careering headfirst into a stack of trays. The canteen erupted into laughter. Rick laughed the loudest by far.

"Stroker!" Blocker snapped. "Come over here and stop messin' about!"

Stroker dusted himself down and hurried back, muttering oaths at everyone laughing. It was enough to turn the air blue.

"You fool," Blocker huffed. "What did you say to the poor girl?"

Stroker, dazed and confused, held his hands up innocently. "I only asked her if she needed a hand."

Rick again chortled heartily for a good minute. "Oh, Gawd blimey," he wheezed, finally, fighting to regain his composure. "I'm glad you came. I hadn't thought about bringing a cabaret." He paused and looked the two men up and down. "What happened to you two? You're a bit old for makin' mud pies, ain't 'cha?"

"A regrettable incident involving a guy rope, a clump of thistles, and a theology professor." Stroker sniffed, still trying to clear out the cobwebs.

"Blimey, you two have all the fun," Rick smirked. "Now, what brings you all the way out here? I thought you had important work back on campus. Run out of papers to put into neat piles?" Rick grinned, stabbed his sausage with a fork and took a bite.

Blocker bristled. Rick had gone too far. It was a

The Nookienomicon

long-running joke on campus that Blocker hadn't done an ounce of work since becoming head of the department. "I'm here, Doctor Romper, to keep an eye on you, and a good thing too. What's all this nonsense I hear about the tomb of Rhum'pee-Phum'pee?"

Rick nearly choked on a mouthful of sausage. "The what?"

"Don't come the innocent with me, Romper. I know all about your ridiculous notions. Cockett told me all about it while we were tangled up in the mud together."

"Blimey, you do work fast, you've only just got here."

"What?" Blocker erupted.

"Fine." Rick sighed. "It's true. I'm not only here to uncover more of the burial mound, but I also believe that further up the gorge lies the tomb of Rhum'pee-Phum'pee. I figured, why bother spending money on two expeditions when we can do two for one, as it were."

"Rubbish," Blocker snorted derisively, a smug grin spreading across his face. "You didn't tell the Dean because you know he wouldn't allow it."

"Not so. The Dean has full faith in my Nookienomicon research." Now it was Rick's turn to be smug.

"Poppycock! It's a forgery, and you know it!" Blocker sneered. If smugness were an Olympic sport, he'd have just won gold.

"I'll have you know, that copy of the Nookienomicon is one-hundred-per-cent legit! It was found by Professor Poker and his team from

The Nookienomicon

Cardiff. They found it buried in a mound just like the Brown Hole out there." He pointed to the flaps at the rear of the tent.

"Brown Hole?" Blocker whispered, his face a mask of shock.

"That's what the locals call it." Rick shrugged. "Anyway, my copy of the Nookienomicon was found in the only other place we have found remains of what Doctor Stiff calls Homo Canis. I paid a pretty penny for it too, so don't you come telling me it's a blasted fake, mate!"

Blocker nodded slyly. "A likely story. I wouldn't put it past you to have made it yourself. Get some animal skins from the local butcher, did you? Get your Auntie Norma to stitch it together, did you? Where was this so-called other mound?"

"Cyn-Y-Lyngus in the Brecon Beacons."

"Cyn-Y-Lyngus? Never heard of it."

"You should get out more, you might learn summat." Rick grinned then nodded towards the table where Vee sat with two other girls. "If you'll excuse me, gentlemen, my sausage is getting cold." Leaving Blocker and Stroker open-mouthed and furious, Rick hurried away with a wide grin plastered across his chops.

It wasn't often that Blocker was at a loss for words, but this was one of those rare occasions. After a few moments of quiet contemplation, he turned to Stroker. "Come along, Willie, we should get on with our erection before it gets dark." Without waiting for a response, he scurried out of the tent and into the crisp April air. Stroker sighed, looked at the mashed potato girl wistfully, then

The Nookienomicon

followed.

Goosing Gorge was nestled deep in the heart of Bodmin Moor, the sort of place that you would never know existed unless you had reason to go there. The fact that the nearby village of Goosing Hole consisted of a couple of ramshackle farms, a handful of crumbling cottages and a public house meant this was unlikely. Unlike the not dissimilar Cheddar Gorge in Somerset, the tourist trade had seemingly overlooked the place despite it being home to several sprawling caverns. Most locals liked it that way and looked down upon their cheesemaking relatives with scorn as if they had somehow sold their souls.

Romper's expedition was sizeable by Gropeham University standards. The Dean was notoriously tighter than a duck's backside so getting him to sign off on a packet of paperclips was unlikely, never mind an operation of this magnitude. Doctor Blocker surveyed the camp and scowled. The fact that Romper had been successful in getting the green light rankled him. He didn't possess Romper's gift of the gab. The old rogue could have sold thistles, heather, and horizontal drizzle to the Scots had he so desired. It made Blocker sick to the guts.

"Let's get it up over there." Blocker pointed over towards a space between a Stormhaven and a large square tent used for cleaning up artefacts.

"Eh?" Stroker looked at Blocker askew.

"The tent!" Blocker was rapidly losing what little patience he had left and nearly bit Stroker's head off. "Go and fetch it from the car. I'll check the ground for stones."

The Nookienomicon

Stroker sighed and flipped Blocker a mock salute while he wasn't looking before skulking off back towards the road. Oblivious, Blocker watched as the girl with the mashed potato on her top ducked into the Stormhaven, already pulling the soiled garment over her head. That was obviously where the students were billeted. He smiled; this was good. Pitching his tent next to it would ensure that none of them got up to any nocturnal nonsense. Better still, he would be right there to see if Romper lived up to his reputation. He was notorious for messing around with his mature students.

Rubbing his hands together to keep out the cold, Blocker ambled over to his chosen pitch. Checking the ground with the side of his boot, he was suddenly drawn towards the examination tent by a familiar voice.

"Oh, no. Not again."

"What's wrong, Professor?" a female voice asked.

"You've gone and stuck the bone in the wrong place again!" the first voice groaned.

"Are you sure? It felt right to me. I couldn't think of anywhere else to stick it."

Blocker gasped. "I know that voice." Hurrying over to the flap, he pulled it aside and poked his head in. "Stiff!" he exclaimed. "What the devil's going on in here?"

Inside the tent, a slender chap with thick round spectacles blinked and stared at Blocker wide-eyed. "Oh, hello!" he smiled. "Fancy seeing you here. This silly girl has gone and stuck my bone in the wrong place again." He pouted and gestured to a

The Nookienomicon

partially assembled skeleton. Emma Rhoyds was standing over it, looking puzzled.

Blocker nearly expired through shock. In the centre of the pelvic bone, sicking up like a flagpole, was a perfectly straight bone. "Miss Rhoyds," he gasped, fighting for air. "Have you been taking cold showers and eating roughage as I told you?"

"Yes, Doctor," she nodded primly.

"Have the dreams stopped?"

"I wouldn't know. I was up all night sneezing and running to the toilet!"

"Never mind all that," Professor Stiff interjected. "What about my skeleton?"

Emma was losing her rag with the whole situation. She grabbed a hammer and a chisel off the workbench. "Don't you worry about your blasted skeleton," she huffed and got ready to polish her second pelvis of the week. She strutted in front of the pelvis and prepared to squat. As her body went downwards, there was a tremendous rip as the too-tight brown cords split down the centre seam, exposing her bright red bloomers.

Both Blocker and Stiff covered their eyes as she shot bolt upright, clamping her hand over the newly formed aperture. Red-faced and sweating, Emma shot out the tent like a whippet with a rocket up its backside. Heading for the Stormhaven, she nearly collided with Stroker, who was absent-mindedly fiddling with a tent pole.

"Oh!" he gasped upon seeing the distressed female. "Do you need a hand?"

Slap!

Back inside, Blocker adjusted his tie and decided

The Nookienomicon

to pretend he hadn't seen Emma Rhoyds' backside. "Anyway... What the devil are you doing here, Stiff?"

"Oh, I'm on loan," Stiff grinned. "The Dean has loaned me out to Romper. Think of me as a rent boy."

Blocker swallowed and looked away. As he glanced at Stiff's paraphernalia, his eyes fell on something he wasn't expecting to see. It was the Nookienomicon. "Good heavens. Is that it? Romper's big discovery." He went to pick it up, but Stiff swatted his hand away.

"Now, now, Doctor. If you are going to fondle it, I must insist that you wear gloves."

"I don't need to fondle it to know that it's a forgery." Blocker sniffed. "Just look at the binding. That face on the cover. It's obviously fake. Any fool can see that."

The Nookienomicon was bound in what looked like human skin and was embossed with a picture of a shocked-looking face, all flared nostrils and puckered lips. Stiff looked at the book, then at Blocker. The resemblance was uncanny. A shiver went down his willowy spine. Reaching into his inside pocket, he retrieved a flask, unscrewed the cap and took a nip. When he was suitably refreshed, he placed the flask on the bench.

All the time Stiff had been distracted, Blocker had been pontificating about the Nookienomicon. "... A child could have made a more convincing forgery out of..."

"Knickers!" Stiff chortled.

"I beg your pardon?"

The Nookienomicon

"You just don't want it to be real so you can sneer at Doctor Romper." Emboldened by the gin in his belly, Stiff was more than a match for Blocker.

"You don't mean to tell me that you believe it's real?"

"I do," Stiff asserted. "And, what's more, I can prove it!" Blocker cocked a sceptical eyebrow as Stiff snapped on a pair of surgical gloves. "What I'm about to show you must go no further than the confines of this tent."

"You can count on me. I'm circumspect."

"Good for you, but can you be trusted?"

Blocker rolled his eyes. "Get on with it, man. I haven't got all night."

Stiff opened the dreaded tome to a page of racy illustrations. The figures involved in what could only be described as lewd activities were hunched and had an almost dog-like aspect. "See the resemblance to the Goosing Gorge skeleton? Considering we have only just discovered this particular branch of evolution, how do you explain that?"

Blocker looked at the drawings. Words failed him.

"The text refers to them as ghuulies. I believe them to be a relative to the mythological Egyptian ghul or the cemetery ghouls of North America. I have been in contact with Professor Peabody at the Miskatonic University in Arkham. He confirms that the bones we have here are similar to the so-called Pickman Skeleton they hold in their museum. Although, there are certain differences."

Blocker was only half-listening. He was

The Nookienomicon

entranced by the drawings. As he stared at the yellowed vellum pages, the figures seemed to dance and move. Their activities created a hypnotic rhythm matched by the increasing roar of the blood in his ears. Blocker screwed up his eyes and pinched the bridge of his nose.

Stiff steadied him as he swayed. "Are you alright, Doctor Blocker?"

"What? Yes, I'm quite alright, why wouldn't I be?" Blocker pulled at his collar and stretched his neck. He'd gone pale and clammy, his eyes were glassy like a beached guppy. Quickly pulling himself together, he reached into his mud-caked tweed jacket and whipped out his copy of *Feeley's Notes*...

"Oh, what's that you've got there?" Stiff's eyes grew wide as he noticed the Bona Books label on the front. He knew all about their special collection that they kept in the backroom. "Is it a good one?"

Blocker was oblivious to the salivating professor. He swiftly thumbed through the notes until he found what he was looking for. It was the passage under the pictures, and it was identical. Blocker swallowed hard. It looked like Romper's Nookienomicon was the real deal after all. "So, what about this Rhum'pee-Phum'pee business? Do you know about that?"

"Oh yes." Stiff waved a hand. "I heard Doctor Romper and Miss Goodthyme arranging a bit for later."

"The tomb of Rhum'pee-Phum'pee, Professor Stiff."

"Oh, I see. Why, yes, I think it's just up the gorge

The Nookienomicon

there. There are existing Roman tunnels dating back to the time of Maximus Raunchius, an early devotee of Nookiemancy. Plus, the locals swear to its existence. Colonel Peacock says he went down there as a boy and came back a man!"

"Locals?" Blocker was still comparing the two texts, desperately trying to prove the Nookienomicon a forgery... he wasn't having any luck.

"At the Boozy Sow Inn at Goosing Hole. I'd, erm, popped in for some refreshments."

"Now, that..." Blocker looked him up and down. Stiff was clearly three-sheets-to-the-wind, as per usual. "I can believe. Could you turn the page, please?"

Stiff did as instructed.

Blocker gasped and started to hyperventilate. His eyes crossed and drifted as he gazed at a centrefold spread of a tentacular monstrosity. It was just as Feeley Senior had described... it was awful.

"Doctor Blocker!" Stiff cried in alarm as he steadied him once again. "You look like you need a stiff one." He reached behind him and grabbed what he thought was his flask. Unfortunately, it was actually a bottle of white spirit that he'd been using to clean his equipment. Blocker nearly choked. He gasped, thumped his chest, then bolted for the tent flap.

Stiff picked up his flask. Holding his gin in one hand and the white spirit in the other, he shrugged, put the gin down and took a swig from the other bottle. "Cor, that puts hairs on your chest!"

Blocker raced outside and nearly mowed down

The Nookienomicon

Professor Stroker who was desperately trying to untangle himself from a guy rope. "I've nearly got it up," he beamed with pride.

It took Blocker a second or two to realise that he was talking about their cramped ridge tent. "Well, don't just stand there. Pack it away. We haven't a moment to lose. I'll meet you back at the car."

Stroker sighed... "Here we go again."

***

The wheels of Stroker's clapped out Morris Marina crunched on the gravel as he pulled into the car park of the Boozy Sow Inn. "So, now you're saying the Nookienomicon is real and that we have to pip Romper to the post?" Stroker's forehead was creased with confusion. For the entirety of the five-minute drive to the tiny hamlet of Goosing Hole, Blocker had ranted and raved about claiming the secrets of nookiemancy and the riches of Rhum'pee-Phum'pee for himself. It was a change in tune so drastic that the poor fellow didn't know whether he was coming or going.

"Yeees. That's precisely what I'm saying. Stiff told me that a Colonel Peacock knows how to get to the tomb. If we beat Romper there, the discovery will be ours, and he'll be little more than a footnote." Blocker smiled smugly, proud of his diabolical plan. "Plus, wouldn't you much rather stay in a nice warm bed than on a flimsy bedroll?"

On this point, Stroker had to agree. On the other, it was pointless arguing. Once Blocker had set his mind to something, no matter how underhand, there

The Nookienomicon

was no shaking him from it. He brought the car to a halt and applied the handbrake. It screeched noisily, making him shudder. Blocker didn't seem to notice. His eyes were glued to the pages of *Feeley's Notes*...

"Fetch our bags, Stroker," Blocker instructed, stepping out into the night. "I'll go and secure us some lodgings." Striding confidently towards the door, he left Stroker mouthing obscenities.

The Boozy Sow was an old coaching inn that dated back to the late twelfth century. A sprawling construction of oak beams and Delabole stone with a giant's fireplace and ivy clinging to its facade. Blocker brushed aside some errant fronds and pushed the door ajar. Warm air and pipe smoke slapped him in the face and gave his nose-hairs a yank. He couldn't help but cough, drawing instant attention to himself.

The bar wasn't busy. Only a handful of locals clustered around the hearth playing cards and dominoes. Most of them were swilling cider that looked like it could strip paint and had beards like rose bushes... and that was just the women. Blocker did his best not to meet their questioning gazes and strutted over to the bar.

A middle-aged woman with a matronly figure stood to the far end, drying a glass with a frayed gingham tea towel. She was gazing into the fire and oblivious to Blocker's presence. He cleared his throat. "Excuse me, madam. I was wondering if you had a room for the night?"

"Oh!" she gasped, her eyes fluttering. "I've always got room for a little one." She sashayed down the bar and rested her chest on the polished

The Nookienomicon

wood. She was dressed in something akin to a Regency serving wench's attire. It had a low neckline revealing a cleavage you could ski down. "It's been ages since I've had the company of a man," she purred, eyeing him wolfishly.

Blocker gulped. "Erm... There's two of us if that's alright."

"Oh, even better. It gets so lonely out here on the moor. Would you like a drink?"

Blocker scanned the pumps before settling on an interesting-looking brew. The picture on the pump showed two terrified-looking miners. "What's that one?"

"Oh, good choice. It's a local brew, a pale ale, named after a miner's superstition. It's called Cornish Knocker."

"Two Cornish knockers then, please." Blocker smiled without thinking.

"Later, dear," the landlady whispered seductively, then gave him a wink and went to pour his drinks.

Blocker felt uncomfortable, like all eyes were on him. So it was something of a relief when Stroker clattered through the door, tripped over a barstool and landed flat on his face. Hurrying to his aid, Blocker told him that he had got them a room and told him to behave himself.

"Here you go, dearies." The landlady smiled, plonking two foaming tankards on the bar.

"Thank you, madam."

"Oh, please, don't stand on ceremony. The name's Betty. Betty Swollocks, but everybody calls me Bet."

The Nookienomicon

Blocker gasped. "I'm not surprised." Noticing her puzzled look, he quickly changed the subject. "Tell me, Bet, do you know a man by the name of Peacock, Colonel Peacock?"

"Of course," Bet smiled. "He's over in the corner enjoying a good rough shag."

"What?" Blocker yelped, turning to look where she was pointing. There was a tiny man with a bushy moustache puffing on a pipe. "Oh, I see. Is there any chance you could introduce us?"

"Sure thing, deary. Oi, Drew... there's a couple of chaps here to talk to you."

Peacock spluttered on a mouthful of smoke before tweaking the end of his moustache. "Send them over, on the double."

Bet rolled her eyes. "You'll have to excuse Colonel Peacock, he still thinks he's in the army... silly old buzzard."

"Come along, man. Quick march!" Peacock bellowed at Stroker, nearly making him drop his ale.

"Coming, Mr Peacock." Blocker grinned, holding his beer in one hand and Stroker's collar in the other.

"It's Colonel!" Peacock exploded.

"Retired." Bet called out primly from the bar.

Peacock harrumphed. "Yes, well. No reason to let standards slip." He turned his attention to Blocker and Stroker. "Sit! Colonel Andrew Peacock, at your service. You may address me as Drew."

"Ah," Blocker took the man's outstretched hand. "Pleased to meet you, Drew Peacock." He stopped

The Nookienomicon

and looked away uncomfortably.

Stroker stifled a snigger.

"Doctor Roger Blocker and Professor Willie Stroker from Gropeham University." Blocker smiled.

"Willie Stroker?" Now it was Peacock's turn to giggle like a schoolboy. "Gropeham University, you say? I wondered when you lot were going to come sniffing around. Had one of your chaps here earlier, tall, gawking fellow."

"Professor Rodney Stiff." Blocker nodded.

"That's the blighter. He came over here earlier looking for shag."

"Eh?" Stroker's eyebrows shot towards the ceiling.

"Me tobacco!" Peacock waved his pipe in Stroker's face, making his nose twitch. "Cheeky devil. Still, he bought me a drink which is more than you two have done."

"My apologies." Blocker waved over to Bet. "A drink for the Colonel, if you'd be so kind."

Bet sighed and rolled her eyes. Drew had a knack for not paying for drinks.

"Now, what can I do for you two gents?"

"I've been told that you are the man to talk to about Rhum'pee-Phum'pee."

"Well, by the looks of things, you don't need my help." Peacock nodded towards Bet, clenched his fist and made a rude gesture as she appeared and set a drink down in front of him. "I think you'll be alright tonight."

"Don't be disgusting!" Blocker exclaimed. "I mean the tomb of Rhum'pee-Phum'pee. Stiff says

191

The Nookienomicon

you've been there?"

Peacock's face flushed, his moustache fluttered, and his eyes glazed over. "Oh, yes. Why do you think I'm so short? I wore myself out. Phwoar!"

"Cor." Stroker grinned. This was starting to sound good after all.

"Could you show us how to get there?"

Peacock thought for a second. "It'll cost you."

Before you could say dodgy dealings, Blocker had whipped out his cheque book and oiled the roguish old colonel's palm. They arranged to meet at first light outside the pub. The three men finished their libations before all deciding to get an early night. Peacock left, and Blocker did his best to avoid the attentions of Bet. Stroker, on the other hand, did the opposite and ended up with another slap for his trouble.

Safely locked away in his room, Blocker had a fitful night...

***

The corridor outside of Doctor Blocker's office seemed to twist and bend as he made his way towards the faculty lounge. There was a foul odour hanging in the air. Damp and musty, with a tang of salt. It reminded him of something, but for the life of him, he couldn't figure out what. Rain lashed the south-facing window as he passed. It sounded vicious out there. Like the wind and rain were making a concerted effort to infiltrate the hallowed halls of Gropeham University.

An electrical fizz nearly made him drop the stack

The Nookienomicon

of papers under his arm as the lights flickered twice before cutting out. Doctor Blocker scowled. "Bloody unions. Not another wretched power-cut?"

"Don't worry, Doctor. I'll sort it," a chipper voice called out from behind him, almost making him leap into the ceiling.

Turning sharply, he spotted a figure reaching out for a light switch. "Cockett, don't, you fool!"

It was too late. Cockett's fingers touched the Bakelite switch, and half of the national grid arced through his body. He screamed and convulsed, his body bucking like an irate mule. Blocker watched in horror as the professor's eyeballs popped and splattered a religious studies timetable.

"Cockett? ... 'ee's 'ad it! ... Wahahahahahaha!"

"Romper?" Blocker turned to look behind him for the source of the echoing laughter. The corridor was enveloped in blackness. There was only a rectangle of sickly green light in the distance. Icy water dripped from above and pooled around his loafers. "What the hell is going on?"

The papers slid from his grasp and fluttered to the floor. Each one was covered in the legend... Doctor Blocker is a fraud.

"Oh, Doctor. Show me where to put the bone."

"Miss Rhoyds?" He turned once again. Emma was nowhere to be seen, neither was Cockett's corpse. In its place was a pile of bloated graveworms. Blocker clamped his bony hand over his mouth and tried not to gag as the wriggling creatures started to form into a humanoid shape. He closed his eyes and shook his head. When he opened them, he was confronted by the hideous

The Nookienomicon

sight of Professor Stroker, stark naked except for a bowler hat, clutching a wilting daffodil.

"Stroker, what's the meaning of this?"

"Where should I put it, Doctor?" He looked at the daffodil with a curious expression.

"Yes, Doctor... where should we put them?" This time, Blocker spun so quickly that he nearly lost his balance. Behind him were several girls from the Archaeology department, Vee and Emma included, all dressed in nurses uniforms clutching a daffodil. "Oh, I see," Vee tittered, pointing at Blocker's lower body. "Bend over, Blocker, there's a good boy!"

Blocker looked down. He was wearing a backless hospital gown. Shrieking with terror, he turned and took off at full pelt past Stroker, who was slowly melting into a pile of green goop. The nurses started to jeer and giggle as they gave chase. The dark tunnel twisted and wound around upon itself until Blocker didn't know if he was going forwards or backwards. One last bend brought him out in front of the aperture with the green light. The nurses were almost on him, their icy fingers tickling his spine and goosing his bare buttocks.

"Quick, Doctor. This way." From the opening, a pair of hands grabbed him and hauled him to safety. A metal door slammed shut, blocking the nurses. "Thank you. Thank you... You? What are you doing here?"

Holding him by the wrists was the landlady of the Boozy Sow, Bet. She was wearing a black satin nightgown. "I've come for you." She grinned, releasing him. "I need your body."

"What? My body? Don't be disgusting. I

The Nookienomicon

wouldn't touch you with Doctor Romper's..." Before he could finish his tirade, Bet opened her nightie to reveal a squirming mass of thick, slippery tentacles.

Blocker screamed.

Bang! Bang! Bang!

"Wakey-wakey, Doctor. It's time to get up."

Blocker tumbled off the bed and landed in a heap. His legs were tangled in the sheets, and his body was soaked in sweat. "Stroker, is that you? I hope you've got trousers on."

"Eh?" came the confused reply. "Colonel Peacock will be here soon. Bet wanted to know if you wanted any breakfast? She said you looked like you could do with a nibble."

"I don't want anything of hers, thank you very much."

"Eh?"

"Oh, never mind. Go downstairs. I'll be down shortly."

Unbeknownst to Doctor Blocker, Stroker flipped him a petulant V-sign through the door before toddling back downstairs.

Blocker rubbed his eyes and untangled himself. "A dream. It was just a dream. Pull yourself together, man. Today, we make history."

***

It was a cold, wet, and miserable morning. The notoriously harsh Cornish weather was doing its best to dampen what little high spirits Blocker had left. In all fairness, he hadn't been with it since he'd joined the rest of the party outside of the Boozy

The Nookienomicon

Sow. They had been hiking for around an hour, and he still hadn't been able to shake the image of the nude Willie Stroker from his mind. He rubbed his hands together and took a sneaky sideways glance at the men alongside him.

Stroker had been waiting outside, cramming a sandwich dripping with brown sauce into his face when Blocker finally came down from his room. It wasn't long before they were joined by a rum looking pair, and no mistake. Colonel Peacock, all five-foot-nothing of him clad in his old army fatigues, was accompanied by a hulking six-foot-six behemoth with a bald pate and heavy brow clad in formal wear. Stroker nearly choked on his streaky bacon.

The man, who Peacock explained was his valet, Winklemeister, hadn't said a word since they left the pub. In stark contrast, Peacock had been droning on about the war for what seemed like an eternity. It had got to the point that Stroker was contemplating throttling him with his own tie.

After a stretch of treacherous terrain heading down a steep valley, Peacock suddenly stopped and shrieked. "Iä Shrug-Nickersoff! Iä the Old Cow of the Woods with a thousand udders!"

"What in God's name are you prattling on about?" Blocker snapped.

Peacock pointed a tremulous finger over towards a line of black bovines that were all staring in their direction. "It's an omen! We must turn back. The stars are against us. The daughters of the Old Cow are stalking us."

"Bullocks," Stroker said flatly.

The Nookienomicon

"I beg your pardon?" Peacock turned bright red with fury.

"Those are bullocks." Stroker shrugged.

Peacock squinted. "Ah, so they are. Well spotted, old chap. Come along then, the entrance is just behind those trees."

Blocker shivered. The trees he indicated were wizened and sick-looking. The sort of trees people used to swear were imprisoned witches... or gods. They seemed to leer at them the closer they got.

"You must be careful when we go down there," Peacock warned as they rounded the trunk of the final tree. "The steps are old and worn. You slip, and you'll come a right cropper." He stopped and pointed under the tangled, tentacle-like roots of the tree. "Down there. It's an old Roman passage, you just need to follow it to the bowels of the gorge. There lies the tomb."

"You?" Blocker asked. "Am I to understand that you're not coming with us?"

"Not on your nelly, old chap." Peacock smoothed his moustache with his thumb and forefinger. "I'm far too old to be dabbling in nookiemancy... sadly."

Stroker genuinely thought the old devil was going to burst into tears. "Nonsense," he smiled, patting him on the shoulder. "You're never too old for a bit of nookiemancy."

Sniffing back the sorrow, Peacock smiled. "You're right. Of course, you are. Come on, chaps, there's not a moment to lose." Stamping his foot like a rampant rabbit, he charged towards the hole and vanished below ground.

The Nookienomicon

Fiddling nervously with an electric torch, Blocker went next, then Stroker, with Winklemeister silently bringing up the rear.

The cramped tunnel snaked deep under Bodmin Moor. The steps were hewn out of solid rock and slippery with aeons of damp and decay. The party moved in silence, concentrating on every step. Peacock had been correct. A misstep could easily prove fatal. After a torturous descent, the stairs levelled out into a low sloping tunnel.

"Yeees." Blocker grinned, running his hand over the rock. "These are definitely Roman tool-marks and no mistake."

"Yes," Stroker agreed. "The phallic carving is a staple of Roman architecture."

"I didn't mean that kind of tool..." He stopped and realised that Stroker was, in fact, correct. He was running his finger along the length of some Roman graffiti. He turned bright red and stuffed his hands in his pockets. "Come along. We are wasting time."

The party continued for what seemed like hours. The tunnel snaked left for a mile, then right, and so on. It was impossible to know just where they were in relation to the rest of Goosing Gorge. Eventually, they neared a junction. Blocker held up his hand and placed his finger to his lips.

Stroker moved up to Blocker's position. "What is it?"

"Listen," Blocker hissed. There was an unnerving scuffling sound. It was heading in their direction.

"What the hell is it?" Stroker was starting to

The Nookienomicon

panic.

"Could be a badger," Peacock declared, whipping out his swagger-stick and flexing it in his hands. "You grab it. I'll give it a seeing to."

"Don't be ridiculous!" Blocker snorted.

It was too late, though. Stroker sprung into the left-hand tunnel with a triumphant "A-ha!"

There was a piercing scream followed by a loud slap! Stroker flew backwards from the force of the blow. It was the canteen girl from the previous evening. She no longer had mashed spud in her cleavage, but she was still in no mood to be grabbed by a dithering old academic. Shoving him aside, she stormed off back the way she came. Stroker stumbled sideways and collided with another figure. It was Doctor Cockett. He happened to be holding an oil lamp in one hand and a crate of blasting charges in the other.

Cockett cracked the back of his head on the wall behind him and instinctively raised his hands to protect himself... letting go of his cargo.

"Run!" Blocker screamed, shoving Stroker and Peacock down the right-hand tunnel. Blocker hadn't moved so fast since he was a teenager. The trio, with Winklemeister lumbering behind, sprinted as fast as they could. It wasn't long before there was a colossal explosion followed by the rumbling of falling rock. The group was hurled forwards into a large chamber. Plumes of dust and debris filled the air, obscuring their vision and choking them. The deafening roar of the explosion left each man with a piercing ringing in their ears.

Eventually, however, the dust settled, and the

The Nookienomicon

ringing faded...

"What the bleedin' 'ell are you playing at, Blocker, you big nit?"

Blocker looked up, blinking grit from his eyes, into the irate face of Rick Romper. "Romper? It was Cockett. He..."

"Cockett? Well, I reckon he's 'ad it if he's under that lot." Rick sniffed. "And what about us. We're bloomin' trapped down here now thanks to you."

"Me?" Blocker bristled as he got to his feet. "It's not my fault the damn fool was carrying a naked flame and a box of explosives. What the devil was he doing?"

"I sent him for the charges as we've found a bricked-up passage, and he wanted better light to examine the pictures on the walls. Can't say I blame him... Phwoar." Rick gestured around the chamber. The walls were covered in lewd carvings.

Blocker's eyes grew wide. "What is this place?" The floor was littered with bones and shreds of clothing. As he turned to take in the room, he nearly tripped over a dog-like skull.

"The tomb of Rhum'Pee-Phum'pee!" Peacock coughed and spluttered as he staggered into the centre of the chamber. "I never thought I'd see it again."

"Who the 'ell is this?" Rick pointed at the diminutive old colonel.

Drew held out his hand in greeting." Colonel Andrew Peacock,"

"Retired," Blocker and Stroker added in unison.

"I showed them the way down here. I never thought I'd see this place again." His face was a

The Nookienomicon

mixture of fear and lust as he wandered off to take in the scenes depicted on the walls.

"Good, ain't they?" Rick grinned. "Like Sodom and Gomorrah with tentacles. I particularly like this one over here. It makes your eyes water just thinkin' about it." Rick was pointing to a depiction of a magnificent tower topped with a plum-coloured dome. "Imagine how hard it was to erect!"

"Rick?" a female voice whined out of the darkness. "Can we get on with it? This stone ain't half cold."

Blocker turned and, for the first time, noticed that in the centre of the chamber was what looked like a chaise longue carved out of solid rock. It was decorated with tentacles and grasping claw-like hands. Lying on top of it, dressed only in a red nightie, was Veronica Goodthyme.

"Quite right, Vee." Rick nodded and started to unbutton his shirt. "There's not a moment to lose. Emma, pass me the book."

Emma Rhoyds held out her hand towards Rick but was intercepted by Colonel Peacock. "Is it? It is!" The man started to whoop and leap from foot to foot. "It's the Nookienomicon!" He spun and capered around the chamber, then...

Bonk!

He was clubbed over the head with a femur. His skull split and his body crumpled.

"I'll take that, thank you very much." Breaking his silence for the first time all day, Winklemeister stooped low and snatched the tome from Peacock's cold dead hands. "It's about bloody time. I've been looking for my book for centuries. I knew it'd come

The Nookienomicon

back here eventually."

"Winklemeister? What's the meaning of this?" Blocker raged. "And what do you mean *your* book?"

"I mean, me old china, that this copy of the Nookienomicon belongs to me. Each nookiemancer has his own Nookienomicon, and this one is mine. Some bugger pinched it from me aeons ago."

"Who the devil are you?"

"The name's Evah-Onthajob. The undying servant of Rhum'pee-Phum'pee."

Blocker gasped. "You knew Rhum'pee-Phum'pee?"

"Not 'alf." Evah grinned. "The filthy old letch. I've met all the great nookiemancers, Uttah Smutt, Maximus Raunchius, you name 'em. That's one good thing about this line of work, you meet all the best people."

"That's all very interesting," Rick groaned with mock tiredness, "but I'm about to perform a great ritual here. Can't all this blather wait?" He was currently in the process of removing his slacks.

"Ahh, so you want to learn the secret of nookiemancy, do you?" Evah-Onthajob grinned. "Very well, I can see from 'ere that you have what it takes." He grinned enthusiastically at Rick's bulging y-fronts.

"That's nice of you to say so. Wuhahaha."

The ancient nookiemancer chuckled. It appeared that he and Romper were kindred spirits. Once he'd finished, he looked around and sniffed. "Yeah, I think we are good to go. Hold on, where's the missus?" He paused and took a large bell from his

The Nookienomicon

pocket and gave it a good clatter.

Stroker yelped as the wall behind him started to rumble before pivoting open.

"Coming, dear." Out of the newly opened door came Betty Swollocks. "Did you find your book then?"

"You?" Blocker hissed. "What? How?"

The smells of smoke and stale beer drifted out of the hidden chamber. Emma shone her torch behind Bet and gasped. "I don't believe it. There's a ruddy beer cellar back here!"

The penny finally dropped. The tomb of Rhum'pee-Phum'pee was directly under the Boozy Sow Inn.

"Enough!" the nookiemancer snapped and opened the dreaded pages of his beloved grimoire. Tipping his bulbous head back, he opened his maw and began to chant. "Ph'nglui mglw'nafh Yog-Sothoth, Rhum'pee-Phum'pee ot bthnkor Azathoth fhtagn!"

The ground started to rumble, and the bones began to move, shake, and rattle. Stroker and Blocker cried out in alarm. Vee and Emma both started to disrobe, seemingly in a trance.

"What the 'ell's he saying?" Rick asked Bet.

"He's asking the Opener of the Way to rip open the fabric of reality and get Azathoth to start the ritual of flesh," she stated as she started to undo her corset. "Everything is prepared."

"Ritual of flesh? I don't think so. Come, Stroker, let's get the hell out of here." Blocker marched towards Bet, prepared to shove her aside. Before he and Stroker could act, however, she opened her garment and unleashed a multitude of writhing pseudopods. One lashed towards Stroker and slapped him across the face. Several more shot out and ensnared Romper.

"You're not going anywhere, dearie. I need your body."

All around the chamber, the bones were coming together and forming a horde of skeletal ghuulies. Blocker gasped. Each one had a bone protruding from its pelvis... it seemed that Emma had been right all along.

Evah-Onthajob chuckled. "I'm sorry, Doc. But you are an important part of the ritual. For Rick here to become a nookiemancer, we must make him his own Nookienomicon. To do that... we need a voyeur." He grinned widely.

All around the chamber, the skeletons started to engage in lewd displays of abandon. Rick embraced Vee. Stroker embraced Emma. The walls, and clothes, melted away as they were surrounded by swirling clouds of chaotic matter. A dizzying cacophony of lustful grunts and the manic piping of unseen instruments rose to a crescendo as the ritual neared its climax.

All the while, Blocker stood and watched in shock, his nostrils flaring and his mouth a perfect O for 'outrage'...

***

The door of the Boozy Sow opened, and a furtive-looking man hurried inside. He looked askew at the glassy-eyed locals, put his mobile

The Nookienomicon

phone in his pocket and made his way to the bar.

"Ahem." He politely cleared his throat to get the attention of the buxom blonde behind the bar. "I have a booking for the weekend in the name of Long. Professor Roderick Long, from Cambridge University."

"Ah, yes. Glad you could make it, Professor. Hold on, I'll just get my hubby." She leaned over the bar, nearly falling out of her top as she did so. "Rick, dear. Mr Long is here to see you."

"Splendid. Good to see you again. Come and join me by the fire."

Professor Long put his bags down next to the bar and walked towards the giant's fireplace. Pulling out a chair, he sat down opposite Rick. "Thank you for giving me this opportunity, Doctor Romper."

"No worries, mate." Rick grinned and pulled out a curious book crafted from the skin of a long-dead academic. "I believe this is what you came to see?"

Long gasped. "Is it? It is. It's the Nookienomicon. May I?" He was already in the process of pulling on some latex gloves.

"Be my guest. And, after you've had a good look, we will be having some friends over for a party in the cellar later. You're more than welcome to join us."

"I'd be honoured." Long smiled, his eyes dancing with delight as he ran his fingers over the face of Doctor Blocker. Frozen forever in an expression of prudish horror.

VIII

The Bone Room
By Ella Ann

"Not again…" she groaned. "I'm so tired of that place."

"What about the Rub Club? We haven't been there in a while," Peter suggested, holding his phone in one large hand and scrolling through the internet with a flippant finger.

"No." Pansy paused. "That place is mostly talk, very little action. Too much chitter-chatter, not enough slap and tickle."

"You're disgusting." Peter's voice was flat, but the corner of his mouth curved into a smirk.

"And you're the only person I know who goes to sex clubs for the drinks."

***

"Just a little more," a gruff voice whispered.

"But it's so sticky," a softer voice whimpered through the dark.

"Well, what did you expect?" a third asked. "A monolith of such massive girth couldn't have been built just anywhere."

"But how does it stay erect in this sludge? I can barely walk."

Several cloaked figures shrugged in the dark and continued on, their rubber boots squirting and spitting through the muck.

The Nookienomicon

"And why do we have to come at night. I can barely see anything under that tiny sliver of light."

"Yeah, aren't we supposed to come out during the gibbous moon?"

"Would you guys shut up," a sharp whisper hissed from the front of the group. "It can't always be a gibbous moon!"

***

"Huh. Never heard of this one before." Peter paused his scrolling to take a sip of his whiskey.

"Go on."

"It's called the Bone Room."

"Oh, spicy."

"But not much on it. Just an address and short description."

"Well, let's hear it."

"It says, '*Welcome to the Bone Room, where the victims of our large tentacled god lay splayed for your viewing pleasure. Come to observe or participate in the exploration, all are welcome.*'"

"Sign me up! I already worship any large tentacle I come across." Pansy jumped to her feet. "Just let me get changed into something less acceptable."

Peter took another absentminded swig of his drink, still focused on his phone, and reclined on Pansy's slightly sticky leather sofa.

"You know," he called to Pansy in the other room, "it's nice they allow onlookers. Some places get weird about the peepers who aren't also pokers, if you know what I mean."

The Nookienomicon

Pansy emerged from the bathroom, wearing her shortest skirt, a bedazzled bra, and her longest, blond wig.

"And how delicious that after, you have to lay about for a bit for everyone to see! Let's go."

The ice in Peter's drink clinked as he finished it off and stood, Pansy's couch moaning in response.

"Maybe they have a copy of the Nookienomicon," Peter said.

"What the hell is that?" Pansy asked, pausing at the door with a raised eyebrow.

"You know, that kinky old sex book we heard about at the Rub Club," Peter winked. "Like Kama Sutra, I think, but better."

***

"Alright, folks, the excavation team should be back from their trip soon."

A substantially built man stood at the front of the dim, candle-lit room, clad in a dark robe. His broad moustache, reminisce of an 80s police officer, wriggled like a thick caterpillar below the low hood shading his eyes.

A hush fell over the shadowy room and its equally shady occupants.

"Now, sales at the Bone Room are up, so we're looking for new and existing members to—"

"Yoohoo, anyone home?"

In unison, twenty-some-odd heads turned toward the curtained doorway just before the main entrance. The warm night air blew in as someone beyond the curtain clunked around the front desk in

The Nookienomicon

what sounded like cumbersome heels.

"Maybe they aren't open on a Wednesday night," a male voice whispered from beyond the curtain. "Not everyone is a thirsty as you."

"Ow, don't elbow me!" the female voice whispered back. "I get it. It's not that clever."

The rather tall, cloaked man who had been interrupted by the intruders strode impatiently toward the heavy, red curtain and yanked it back to reveal a scantily clad couple standing at the front desk.

"Oh, hello," the blonde woman smiled widely. "Is this the Bone Room?" Stepping forward, she peeked behind the cloaked man to peer into the room beyond.

"Babe, look," her male companion nudged, also peeking behind the strange bouncer. "They started their boning activities without you."

With startling abruptness, the tall man before them pulled the curtain closed behind him and spoke in a deep, stern voice.

"How do you know about that?"

"No need to worry," the man said, placing a confident hand on his shoulder. "We're no strangers to these types of activities and the precautions you have to take to prevent the not-so-openminded from poking about, and not in a good way."

Letting out a good-natured chuckle, he removed his hand from the stranger's shoulder.

"Poking about, yes," the cloaked man said with a slow smile, "but not for bones."

"Well, we can assure you," the woman winked, "we are here for all the 'bones' we can get."

The Nookienomicon

After a moment of silence, the large man in the black hood unknit his brow and stood aside for the couple to move past him and the curtain, before returning to his place at the front of the room.

***

"Velvet?" Pansy whispered as the heavy fabric brushed across her arm. "They *are* kinky."

"I just hope that guy's equipment is as thick as his moustache," Peter whispered back as they entered a dimly lit room and stood off to the side.

The dozens of dark eyes turned away as they followed the bouncer to a table at the front of the room.

"Is that a candelabra?" Pansy snickered. "We've never gotten so fancy with our wax-play before."

"Maybe it's so they can drip more of it in one go?" Peter shrugged.

"Oh, that's smart. Remind me to order one when we get home later."

"Ladies and gents," the man at the front of the room began, "talk about fast manifestation."

Soft chuckles filled the room.

"Here, I was just saying how we were looking for more members for our boning expeditions, and then comes a knock at the door."

He gestured toward Peter and Pansy with an upward palm as if offering the group a delicious meal.

"Allow me to introduce myself," the man continued. "I am Lord of Bones, Leader of the Esoteric Order of Gagon."

The Nookienomicon

"Oh, I'm so ready to get my gag on," Pansy whispered.

"I wish I knew they were into this cloak business. I could have come naked under a trench coat."

"I know," Pansy replied, "they really ought to get a website. I mean, I'm into the whole underground thing, but that would have been fun. I could have worn that red rain jacket with matching rubbers."

"You mean galoshes," Peter smiled.

"Those too." Pansy winked. "Do you think they give us naughty titles, too? Or maybe we have to pick our own as part of this whole roleplay they got going on?

"Excuse me," Lord of Bones interrupted, an agitated edge to his deep voice. "Can we have our new members announce themselves, please?"

"Yes, of course," Pansy excitedly stepped forward. "I'm Pansy," she declared, pausing momentarily. "Mistress of Boning."

"Uh, yes," Peter followed, taking a step forward. "And I'm Peter, Master Boner."

The deep frown of the heavily moustached man before them suddenly tweaked itself into a smile.

"Ah, yes, you said you've belonged to such an establishment before?" Lord of Bones asked. "Is that where you earned such titles?"

"Yes, our most esteemed Bone Lord," Pansy replied, "I can assure you, our titles are well-earned."

Peter stifled a snicker as Pansy erupted in a sudden coughing fit that sounded quite like poorly masked laughter.

The Nookienomicon

"Well, then, a most hearty welcome from us all," the Bone Lord replied, his eyebrows high in apparent surprise.

"Welcome, Mistress of Boning and Master Boner," the congregation said in robotic unison.

"Please, find yourselves a pillow or two and be seated," the Bone Lord instructed.

Peter and Pansy found the nearest pillows and lowered themselves awkwardly onto the ground.

"No wonder they come in robes," Pansy whispered to Peter after struggling to get comfortable in her skirt and bulky heels. "And what's with all the velvet? I can already tell my arse is going to be chafed before the night is out."

***

"As I was saying. Our Boning Team will be back soon, and I would like some volunteers to go on the next trip."

"Now we're talking," an excited voice at the back of the room whispered.

"Pansy, Mistress of Boning, are you volunteering?" Lord of Bones asked, again taken by surprise by this rambunctious woman.

"Why, yes, your eminence," Pansy half grunted as she struggled to her feet. "I'm always up for a boning trip. Besides, if I sit on this velvet pillow any longer before you get me into one of those sweet capes, no one is gonna want to see what I got going on down there."

"And can I assume you'll be volunteering as well, Peter, Master Boner?"

The Nookienomicon

"You got it," Peter replied, offering the Lord a finger gun and a wink.

***

As if on cue, a rather disheveled lot entered through the far end of the room, carrying sacks filled with protruding, nubbed objects.

"A warm welcome to our fearless Boners, and best wishes to our outgoing team."

"Look!" Pansy dropped her voice so as not to be heard by the Bone Lord. "Sacks full of *equipment*."

As Pansy, Peter, and several others were ushered out of the room, one of the returning Boners handed Peter a sack of smaller size.

"Aw man," Peter muttered. "I got a bloody book."

"Maybe it's the Nookienomicon," Pansy offered, rubbing his arm consolingly.

The small group continued down a narrow corridor and into another candle-lit room, where the Bone Lord handed everyone a small cup of wine.

Peter looked down at his plastic cup in disappointment.

"I normally go for the harder stuff. You got anything else?" he asked, smiling genially.

The Bone Lord returned his smile and placed a small pill in Peter's hand.

"It's to wash down this, my son."

"Uh, thanks, Bone Daddy," Peter replied, tentatively closing his hand around the pill and raising an eyebrow at Pansy as she received hers.

"It is a trip on multiple planes, you see," Lord of

The Nookienomicon

Bones stated to the group as Peter and Pansy moved to the back. "As our newcomers probably know, different Orders choose different methods to reach the lands of the Old Ones, including the great monolith of Cthulhu, mightily erected by skilled hands."

"What the hell is he talking about?" Peter whispered close to Pansy's ear.

"I don't know, something about giving a hand job. What'd you do with your pill?"

"Dropped it in this bookbag. I'm going to save it for the orgy. This guy talks so much, I don't want it to wear off before then."

"Good idea," Pansy whispered, digging into her bedazzled bra. "Keep mine, too. I don't want to lose it when we strip down."

"Master, Mistress, and Boners, please place this solemn pearl upon your tongue, and raise your glasses."

"To the Old Ones!" the group chanted, followed by an awkward silence, interrupted only by gulping.

"I think they're talking about how people back in the 70s used to have orgies and stuff like that," Pansy said in response to Peter's raised eyebrow.

***

It was nearly midnight, and the small group had been walking for almost half an hour. None of the cloaked members of the Order spoke, padding through the mucky marshlands with their shovels in hand.

Trailing behind the group, Peter and Pansy tittered and joked about how they were about to be murdered by a cult of sex-addicts.

"That's the reason they didn't give either of us a shovel," Peter chuckled. "All you got was a bunch of empty sacks, probably for our chopped-up limbs, and all I got was a damn book."

"Let's open it and look through the different positions while we walk. That way, we're prepared when this damn orgy finally starts."

"Too late," Peter replied.

Just ahead, the group halted before a dead, charred tree that looked like a gnarled hand reaching up at the crescent moon.

As Peter and Pansy approached, they saw one of the members standing in front of the tree, and the rest formed a semi-circle around it.

"Behold!" the young man at the front of the group called out. "The great monolith of Cthulhu."

Peter snorted out a laugh.

"These people are so high on acid."

"If we came out here for any reason other than having sex against that sad lightning victim, I'm gonna be pissed," Pansy said with an agitated sigh.

"Let us harvest the victims of our great God, extract the bones of the once-living from this infernal sludge."

"Uhh, babe…" Peter said, his voice trailing off.

But Pansy didn't look, her face frozen, gaze locked on something in the distance.

"Tombstones…" she whispered. "There's a graveyard past that tree."

"Blimey," Peter whispered.

The Nookienomicon

"Are you thinking what I'm thinking?" Pansy asked. But when she finally looked at Peter, he wasn't looking at the graveyard. Staring down at the book in his hands, he held it up so Pansy could read the cover.

"Neck, what…?" she whispered. "What does it say?"

"Necro something," Peter hissed. "Necro… As in *necro*philia. These people have sex with corpses!"

"Oh my god, they brought us out here to have an orgy with dead people?! That must be what the shovels are for."

"No, those are skeletons. You can't have sex with a skeleton!" Peter dropped the book and ducked behind the nearest bush, pulling Pansy with him. "They brought us out here to kill us with shovels and muck about with our dead bodies!"

"Or they're going to strangle us and then use the shovels to bury us. But wait," Pansy paused, "what are the sacks for?"

"Pansy, for fuck's sake, who cares?! We got to get the hell out of here. Give me your wig."

"What? Why? It's not a magic wig."

"Just give it to me!"

"I mean, it works magic, don't get me wrong," she whispered, removing pins quickly from her hairline. "But not, you know, teleportation kind of magic."

Shaking out her naturally black locks, she handed the blonde wig to Peter.

"Alright. These people are high as a rogue bloody balloon. Look…" Peter paused, and they

The Nookienomicon

peered around their protective bush. "That guy is still going on about that dead tree."

"Ridiculous." Pansy's eyes squinted through the dark. "I'll bet your branch is harder than those."

"Focus, Pansy. Here's the plan. I'm going to put your wig on this bush. They're so high, they'll think we're over here. Or better yet, they'll think the bush is just part of you."

"Hey! My bush has never been *that* big."

"I don't know. Your 80s phase was pretty intense." Peter chuckled and kissed Pansy on the cheek. "And if we get out of this alive, I want to see it like that again."

"Only for you," Pansy whispered, grabbing his hand.

"Alright, on the count of three. One..." Peter counted.

"Two," Pansy continued.

"Three," they whispered in unison before running off into the murky dark.

***

Lord of Bones sat quietly in the candlelight, cleaning dirt off the skeletons recovered during the first expedition of the evening. In a kind of meditative state, the rest of the Order sat about the room, doing the same.

"How much shall we charge for this one?" one of many cloaked members of the Order asked. "Full female. The bones are strong."

"A couple thousand, perhaps. But I'll need to look at it in better lighting tomorrow," Lord of

The Nookienomicon

Bones replied. "For now, you can take it to the Bone Room."

Just then, he heard the front door of the shop open for the second time that night.

"I thought I asked someone to lock that door," he mumbled to himself.

"Hullo?" a voice called out as a man wearing tight shorts breezed past the curtain. "Is this the Bone Room?"

Spotting the skeletal remains strewn about the cloaked figures, the nearly nude man abruptly stopped.

"Oh. Those are," the man paused to look around, "actual bones."

"As opposed to?" the Lord asked, agitated.

"You know, a boom boom room." The man put his hands behind his head and thrust his hips towards the Lord of Bones.

"Cthulhu almighty, we need a different name."

The Nookienomicon
Author Bios:

Robert Poyton is the founder of Innsmouth Gold, set up as an outlet for his music and literary projects. A long-time fan of weird fiction and Sword and Sorcery, Robert is a professional musician, writing and performing with garage-horror band The Phobias. He is also an experienced martial arts instructor, having published a wide range of books and films on Chinese and Russian arts. Born and raised in East London, Robert now lives in rural Bedfordshire, where he enjoys making a noise and swinging sharp objects around.
www.innsmouthgold.com

S.O. Green (they/them) is a genre-fluid writer and editor living in the Kingdom of Fife with husband, John. Author of the post-apocalyptic novelette, Sin Chaser, published by Eerie River Publishing, as well as over 70 works with imprints including Dragon Soul Press, Black Ink Fiction and Nordic Press. They won 3rd Place in the British Fantasy Society's Short Story Contest 2018. Writer, vegan, martial artist, gamer, occasionally a terrible person (but only to fictional people).
thebasementoflove.blogspot.com

Chris Hewitt lives in the beautiful garden of England and in the odd moment he's not walking the dog, he pursues his passion for writing fiction. With horror, fantasy, and science-fiction stories published in dozens of anthologies.
You can keep up with Chris' writing at:
Facebook: https://www.facebook.com/chris.hewitt.writer
Twitter: @i_mused_blog
Blog: http://mused.blog

Beth W. Patterson was a full-time musician for over two decades before diving into the world of writing, a process she describes as "fleeing the circus to join the zoo". She is the

The Nookienomicon

author of the books *Mongrels and Misfits*, *The Wild Harmonic*, and a contributor to over seventy anthologies.

Patterson has performed in twenty countries across five continents. Her playing appears on over two hundred albums, singles, soundtracks, commercials, and voice-overs (including eight solo albums of her own). More than a hundred of her compositions and co-writes have been released. She studied ethnomusicology at University College, Cork in Ireland and holds a bachelor's degree in Music Therapy from Loyola University New Orleans.

Beth has occasionally worn other hats as a body paint model, film extra, minor role actor, recording studio partner, record label owner, producer, and visual artist. She is a lover of exquisitely stupid movies and a shameless fangirl of the band Rush. She lives in New Orleans with her husband Josh Paxton, jazz pianist extraordinaire, and tours extensively with Scottish fiddle champion Seán Heely. You can find her at www.bethpattersonmusic.com

David Green is a writer of the epic and the urban, the fantastical and the mysterious. With his character-driven dark fantasy series Empire of Ruin, or urban fantasy noir Hell in Haven featuring the snarky PI Nick Holleran, David takes readers on emotional, action-packed thrill rides.

Hailing from the north-west of England, David now lives in County Galway on the west coast of Ireland with his wife and train-obsessed son. When not writing, David can be found wondering why he chooses to live in places where it constantly rains.

www.davidgreenwriter.com

Callum Pearce is a Dutch storyteller, originally from Liverpool. He is mostly a fiction writer. He has been published multiple times across a variety of platforms.

A Lover of the magical as well as the macabre. He lives in a foggy, old fishing town in the Netherlands with his husband, a couple of cat shaped sprites and a trickster god in the shape of a dog.

Featured in lots of drabble collections and anthologies or online with stories for adults and young people. He has also written several factual articles for an LGBTQ+ lifestyle and a music website. Check his pages for things that are available now, coming soon or free to read online.

Callumpearcestoryteller.com
twitter.com/Aladdinsane79
www.facebook.com/calmpeace13

Tim Mendees is a rather odd chap. He's a horror writer from Macclesfield in the North-West of England that specialises in cosmic horror and weird fiction. A lifelong fan of classic weird tales, Tim set out to bring the pulp horror of yesteryear into the 21st Century and give it a distinctly British flavour. His work has been described as the love-child of H.P. Lovecraft and P.G. Wodehouse and is often peppered with a wry sense of humour that acts as a counterpoint to the unnerving, and often disturbing, narratives.

Tim has had over eighty published short stories and novelettes along with six stand-alone novellas and a short story collection.

When he is not arguing with the spellchecker, Tim is a goth DJ and a co-host of the Innsmouth Book Club podcast. He currently lives in Brighton & Hove with his pet crab, Gerald, and an army of stuffed octopods.

https://timmendeeswriter.wordpress.com/
https://tinyurl.com/timmendeesyoutube

Ella Ann enjoys reading and writing in a wide array of genres. Born and raised on the West Coast of the United States, she currently resides in Southern California. While attending graduate school, she found her passion in creative writing. She types most of her stories late at night, with a snoozing pup near her feet.

The Nookienomicon

The Nookienomicon

Also from Red Cape Publishing

Anthologies:

Elements of Horror Book One: Earth
Elements of Horror Book Two: Air
Elements of Horror Book Three: Fire
Elements of Horror Book Four: Water
A is for Aliens: A-Z of Horror Book One
B is for Beasts: A-Z of Horror Book Two
C is for Cannibals: A-Z of Horror Book Three
D is for Demons: A-Z of Horror Book Four
E is for Exorcism: A-Z of Horror Book Five
F is for Fear: A-Z of Horror Book Six
G is for Genies: A-Z of Horror Book Seven
H is for Hell: A-Z of Horror Book Eight
I is for Internet: A-Z of Horror Book Nine
J is for Jack-o'-Lantern: A-Z of Horror Book Ten
K is for Kidnap: A-Z of Horror Book Eleven
L is for Lycans: A-Z of Horror Book Twelve
M is for Medical: A-Z of Horror Book Thirteen
N is for Nautical: A-Z of Horror Book Fourteen
It Came from the Darkness: A Charity Anthology
Out of the Shadows: A Charity Anthology
Castle Heights: 18 Storeys, 18 Stories
Sweet Little Chittering
Unceremonious
The Nookienomicon

The Nookienomicon

Short Story Collections:

Embrace the Darkness by P.J. Blakey-Novis
Tunnels by P.J. Blakey-Novis
The Artist by P.J. Blakey-Novis
Karma by P.J. Blakey-Novis
The Place Between Worlds by P.J. Blakey-Novis
Home by P.J. Blakey-Novis
Short Horror Stories by P.J. Blakey-Novis
Short Horror Stories Vol.2 by P.J. Blakey-Novis
Keep It Inside & Other Weird Tales by Mark Anthony Smith
Everything's Annoying by J.C. Michael
Six! By Mark Cassell
Monsters in the Dark by Donovan 'Monster' Smith
Barriers by David F. Gray
Love & Other Dead Things by Astrid Addams

Novelettes:

The Ivory Tower by Antoinette Corvo

Novellas:

Four by P.J. Blakey-Novis
Dirges in the Dark by Antoinette Corvo
The Cat That Caught the Canary by Antoinette Corvo
Bow-Legged Buccaneers from Outer Space by David Owain Hughes
Spiffing by Tim Mendees
A Splintered Soul by Adrian Meredith
Scavengers of the Sun by Adrian Meredith

The Nookienomicon

Novels:

Madman Across the Water by Caroline Angel
The Curse Awakens by Caroline Angel
Less by Caroline Angel
Where Shadows Move by Caroline Angel
Origin of Evil by Caroline Angel
Origin of Evil: Beginnings by Caroline Angel
The Vegas Rift by David F. Gray
The Broken Doll by P.J. Blakey-Novis
The Broken Doll: Shattered Pieces by P.J. Blakey-Novis
South by Southwest Wales by David Owain Hughes
Any Which Way but South Wales by David Owain Hughes
Appletown by Antoinette Corvo
Nails by K.J. Sargeant

Art Books:

Demons Never Die by David Paul Harris & P.J. Blakey-Novis
Six Days of Violence by P.J Blakey-Novis & David Paul Harris

The Nookienomicon

Follow Red Cape Publishing

www.redcapepublishing.com
www.facebook.com/redcapepublishing
www.twitter.com/redcapepublish
www.instagram.com/redcapepublishing
www.pinterest.co.uk/redcapepublishing
www.patreon.com/redcapepublishing
www.ko-fi.com/redcape
www.buymeacoffee.com/redcape